DIE YOU
DOUGHNUT
BASTARDS

PRAISE FOR CAMERON PIERCE

"Like Williams S. Burroughs on crack!"
—**THOMAS F. MONTELEONE**, *New York Times* bestselling author

"Pierce is one of the weirdest, most imaginative writers around."
—**LLOYD KAUFMAN**, director of *The Toxic Avenger* and *Poultrygeist*

"Dr. Seuss meets David Cronenberg."
—**CARLTON MELLICK III**

"Before he goes gently into that weird night by spontaneously combusting, Pierce seems hellbent on writing his fill of Bizarro lit. His tales include many standard tropes, like pickles and pancakes falling in love, or ass-shaped goblins who abduct children for slave labor and eating, or flying Biblical sharks. It's a scene."
—**CRACKED.COM**

THE PICKLED APOCALYPSE OF PANCAKE ISLAND

"Weird, wicked, wonderful."
—**PIERS ANTHONY**, *New York Times* bestselling author

"A most definite fractured fairy tale. (And my favorite book title of all time.)"
—**S. G. BROWNE**, author of *Breathers* and *Fated*

LOST IN CAT BRAIN LAND

Winner of the Wonderland Book Award, Best Collection of 2010

"These mostly first-person (and occasionally second-person) narratives (dis)locate their characters in worlds too strange to be fiction. Check it out."
—**NICK MAMATAS**, author of *Bullettime* and *Sensation*

"This is the strangest collection I've ever read. It seems to have come from some other place."
—**ALAN M. CLARK**, World Fantasy Award winner

CTHULHU COMES TO THE VAMPIRE KINGDOM

"Just about every page is filled with the spawn of a delightfully mad dreamer."
—INNSMOUTH FREE PRESS

"A bizarro fever-dream tale of vampire lovers attempting to summon a hamburger and LOLCat-obsessed Cthulhu to destroy their doomed undersea kingdom. Including a Necronomicon that is really a unicorn coloring book, *Cthulhu Comes to the Vampire Kingdom* is sure to annoy Lovecraftian purists, but made me laugh out loud at many turns."
—ROSS E. LOCKHART, editor of *The Book of Cthulhu*

ASS GOBLINS OF AUSCHWITZ

"I am slightly afraid of it. It looks kind of contagious."
—WARREN ELLIS

"In an era when very little remains shocking, Pierce might have actually managed to create a genuinely disturbing work of fiction, the literary equivalent of *Schindler's List* rewritten by the Marquis De Sade and filmed as a Tim Burton animated feature."
—THE GUARDIAN

"Truly disgusting! A fascinating mix of William Burroughs, David Cronenberg and Lenny Bruce if you were to take all three and drop them into a blender. Pierce is a writer with a truly warped imagination."
—KEITH J. CROCKER, director of *Blitzkrieg: Escape From Stalag 69*

GARGOYLE GIRLS OF SPIDER ISLAND

"If you were to take everything horror writers typically shy away from and mush it into one streamlined novel, you might get something like splatterpunk adventure tale Gargoyle Girls of Spider Island. Expect to see gruesome shark attacks, pirate hijackings and plenty of multi-vaginal tentacle monsters during your travels, while action, sex, and laughs compete for page space. Seriously."
—RUE MORGUE

DIE YOU DOUGHNUT BASTARDS

Eraserhead Press
205 NE Bryant Street
Portland, Oregon 97211

www.eraserheadpress.com
www.bizarrocentral.com

ISBN: 978-1-62105-055-1

CONTENTS

Champions always die with a smile on.

DIE YOU DOUGHNUT BASTARDS

I

When you're hung over, can't remember the night before, and count yourself among the last two people alive in a world overrun by flesh-eating doughnut bastards, life is shit.

Yes, doughnuts.

Breakfast sweets rule the world.

And no, I'm not getting out of bed.

Ira will be pissed, but Ira is always pissed.

Fuck her. Fuck her if she won't fuck me.

I need to sleep. I'll kill anyone who wakes me. I will kill Ira and kill myself and my dead body will sleep with her dead body.

My head is throbbing. My liver aches.

I often imagine entire conversations between Ira and I where I confess to her just how much I regret the things I do.

But we don't talk about those things. I keep quiet most of the time. I shut myself away.

I'd cut out my tongue for a reason to live.

We're the last two humans left alive. She thinks there must be someone else out there, but what does she know? Ira is full of shit.

I can't fall asleep again. The doughnut birds outside my window are screaming. The doughnut birds won't let me sleep.

I need to take a crap, but I'm exhausted and bloated, nauseated to the gills. I roll onto my belly and shit myself. It's my own business if my shit clings to the backs of my legs. Cleanliness is shit. I'm not made of sugar. I'm not a fucking doughnut creep. I'm a human fucking being, and that means I'm ugly.

I stumble into the bathroom. Splash cold water on my face. Faded graffiti covers the walls. A pink napkin is stuck to the bathroom mirror.

OUT OF TP, FUCKER. - IRA

Ira and I wouldn't be living together if it wasn't for the end of the world. I'm only obsessed with her because I'm lonely. Any time I fail at anything or forget to bring something home from a dumpster raid, she gets pissed and sometimes hits me. She yells and throws things. She refuses to acknowledge that she fails and forgets just as often.

I don't bother brushing my teeth. We share a toothbrush and right now I'm too pissed at Ira to share her germs.

I put on the same black t-shirt and starchy green pants that I've worn for the past week. I don't own any socks right now. My only pair went missing last week. I probably set them on fire.

The walls of this house are covered in black mold. You can smell it. Can't avoid it.

I breathe in mold spores and think of a book bound in chocolate flesh and written in raspberry blood.

I slip on my boots, grab my plastic blue raincoat, and comb my fingers through my greasy hair. Last night's whiskey sloshes around in my paunch.

I reach into my pocket and pull out a cigarette pack. I open the pack and it's empty. I do this out of habit. I've carried this crumpled pack around for weeks. It's a fucked-up thing to be out of cigarettes.

The phone rings.

The world ended and we still have telephones.

Ha!

I pick up the phone and stick the mouthpiece inside my bottom lip. Electricity crackles on my tongue, shocking the enamel off my gnarled teeth.

"Hello?" I rub my jaw, holding the telephone in the other hand. Even basic greetings are painful.

"Why the fuck aren't you awake yet?" Ira asks.

"Am I dreaming?"

"You dipshit."

"Sorry, I overslept. Where are you? Are you coming home?"

"I'll pick you up in five minutes."

"Where are we going?"

"Wait outside for me."

Our connection goes dead.

I remove the mouthpiece and slam down the telephone.

If I wrote a pop song, I would call it "Your friend is an alcoholic amputee and her anti-depressants turn her pussy into sour apples, which depresses her more than the depression she is battling, so why don't you stop doing cunnilingus with that chocolate bar and stick it in your fritter friend already?"

I guess that's why I don't write pop songs.

Outside, I'm shivering.

The sky dumps sugar and a few stray chocolate chips.

Too bad happy people have gone extinct.

I wonder if I'll end up being the last human alive.

Ira will arrive soon. She's got this submarine car. It is slow and it is quiet.

As I wait for her, I feel an abstract sense of wonder about cats and dogs.

It's fucking cold out here.

The bacon storm will be a bitch tonight. Bacon lightning greases everything—the streets, our skin, the air. When it strikes in conjunction with heavy sugarfall, that's the worst, the most dangerous. We stumble around half-blind, reeking of candied bacon.

5

Ira pulls up and starts honking.

I hurry to her submarine car, which looks like a fat white worm.

I open the passenger door.

"Back seat!" she screams.

"Sorry," I say, "I forgot."

I open the passenger-side back door.

Ira is bossy, disagreeable, and selfish. I've been in love with her since we met. I don't care that I love her out of loneliness. She is beautiful.

She glares at me in the mirror. Her blonde hair looks like a tumbleweed.

"Hi," I say.

"Do you want to talk about last night?" she asks.

"Last night..."

"The beer bottles. On our lawn. In the shape of a fucking heart."

"How did you know it was me?"

"You're the only other person in the world."

"Then why do we keep looking for survivors?"

Ira ignores my question. "Do you know how many doughnut birds you attracted? You could have attracted the doughnut people. We could be dead right now."

"You're right. We could be."

"Fuck you," she says.

She turns on the stereo and cranks up the heater all the way.

I say nothing as cold sweat drips down my face and bleeds into my palms.

"So where are we going?" I ask.

"A house on the edge of town. I finally mapped out where that radio signal is coming from."

Ira's primary obsession is finding other people. She has yet to track down a single survivor, but she'll spend hours every day searching for signs in the greasy wasteland. We never find anyone. We will never find anyone.

"Will it be different this time?"

Ira says nothing.

Most of the time, radio signals turn out to be ghosts. Not real ghosts, but leftover energy deposits or something. Ira has a funny way of explaining it. She compares the phenomenon to dead radios coughing.

"Will we get back before nightfall?"

"We might have to camp out."

"What if the house isn't secure?"

Ira says nothing.

A while later, we pull up in front of a two-story house.

We climb out of the submarine car and edge up the walkway. The front door is locked, so Ira removes the lock-picking kit attached to her utility belt. She picks the lock in less than a minute.

She opens the door, her doughnut-smashing hammer raised in case a doughnut person is waiting on the other side to attack.

A man leaps out from behind a sofa and fires a gun. Before I understand what's happening, Ira drops to the floor, her face a bloody hole, and I'm picking up the hammer and charging the man.

The man tries to pistol whip me as I crush his feet under repeated hammer blows. Finally, he throws the gun aside. He must've used his last shot on Ira.

I stand, panting, and move away from the murderer. I look at the wall behind him, too enraged to look directly at him. I should be sad about Ira, but all I feel is anger encased like a tumor in a hunk of meat. I should be crying, but I can't. And all of a sudden I realize I never needed Ira. She's as worthless as anyone in the history of the world. She was right about one thing though: we were not alone in this world. I must admit I'm surprised.

"Get up," I say.

"But my feet are broken."

"Get up or I'll break your arms."

The man stands, agonizingly.

As he rises, his toes regenerate.

His toes are maple bars now. He is infected. I toss Ira's doughnut-smashing hammer aside, suddenly afraid of it. I'm shocked there's enough doughnut disease clinging to the mallet to infect a man. Cleanliness is shit, sure, but did Ira ever clean the hammer? If that thing had brushed against an open wound, she or I could have turned into a doughnut person like this guy.

Then I realize she probably liked having that power over me.

"Do you have any nails?" I ask the man with maple bars for toes.

"Yeah, somewhere."

"Find them. Get a hammer as well. Your gunshot is going to attract doughnuts. I want you to nail up the door and windows as soon as possible."

"Can't I use your hammer?"

"Do what I say or I will fucking kill you."

As he leaves the room, I wonder if I have made a mistake, if he is going to return with another gun so he can kill me too. I kick the empty pistol under the sofa, close the front door, and pace up and down the room, eager for the piece of shit to return.

I feel afraid.

I cannot kill him because then I'll be alone.

I cannot be alone.

II

The bacon storm is rolling in. We hear the grease and sugar beat against the roof and windows. "Your feet smell. Put your shoes on or I'll fry you," I tell the man with maple bars for toes. He has nailed two tables and many chairs over the doors and windows.

"Unfortunately, that's all," he says.

A pounding on the door startles us. The doughnut people are attacking. We press close together, forgetting for a moment that we hate each other.

"I don't care if there are no more chairs," I shout. "Nail more chairs to the door or I'll fucking fry you."

"But there aren't any more chairs!" he says.

"Do you want to go in the deep fryer?"

"No."

"Then nail some more chairs to the door."

The man with maple bars for toes picks up the hammer and a handful of nails. He goes through the motions of nailing chairs to the door.

"Good job nailing those chairs," I say. "You're a carpenter of invisible things. Keep it up. I'm going into the kitchen for a snack. And put your shoes on. Or I'll cut you."

He looks at me with an expression of tired panic.

I go into the kitchen, feeling victorious because he is more afraid than I am. He is afraid because he has killed the girl I loved and, knowing how he has destroyed me, he knows I'm not afraid to destroy him.

I don't know his name and I don't care.

His life is over when I say it is.

There's a coconut in the refrigerator and I pull it out.

In the living room, the man with maple bars for toes has his back turned to me. He's totally absorbed in nailing invisible chairs to the door.

I throw the coconut at his head.

The coconut hits him in the head, falls to the tiled floor, and breaks open.

He drops the hammer and grabs his head, groaning in pain.

"That happened to me once," I say. "Now we share a mutual pain. Do you want a coconut sandwich?"

"No," he says.

"Okay, how about a burrito?"

"No," he says.

"You're going to exhaust yourself."

"I'm not hungry." He's still rubbing his head.

9

"I will make you a coconut sandwich and you will eat it, you murderous son of a bitch. Now keep nailing chairs to the door. If the doughnuts break into this house, I will fucking kill you."

"Shouldn't I be nailing things to less secure places? I mean, the entire dining set is already nailed to the front door, plus all these invisible chairs."

"What the fuck is your problem?" I shout.

I walk over to him as if I am going to fight him. I pick up the two halves of coconut and return to the kitchen, muttering, "Kill his ass." I say it loud enough so that he can hear me but thinks I'm talking to myself. That's the best way to hurt someone. Welcome them into your private thoughts, then trap them there with a mirror that projects only the most negative outlook.

The bread is moldy so I don't make sandwiches. I microwave two frozen burritos instead.

I go into the front room with the burritos and a bottle of hot sauce. I sit on the couch, the plate of burritos on my lap.

"Thanks," says the man with maple bars for toes.

"Thanks for what?"

"For making me a burrito. I realized I was hungry after all."

"I didn't make you a burrito. These burritos are not for you."

"Well are there any more?"

"Sorry, these were the last two."

"Okay," he says, and sits down on the ground.

"There's a frozen lasagna in there."

He perks up. "Really?"

"Yeah, but I ran it through the garbage disposal."

"Oh." He looks sad. "Lasagna is my favorite food."

"Just kidding."

He perks up. "You didn't actually run the lasagna through the garbage disposal, did you? That was just a joke, right?"

"There was never any lasagna," I say.

"Oh." He looks sad again. "I thought maybe you brought some."

"While you were shooting my friend in the face, did you happen to see me holding a box of frozen lasagna?"

"No."

"Then why don't you put your shoes on like I fucking told you?"

"My shoes don't fit anymore. My toes are longer than they used to be."

I eat half a burrito in one bite and I talk with my mouth full. "Well they fucking smell bad. And they're ugly."

"Hey, do you hear that?"

"But I guess you're just an ugly person."

"Listen up."

"Getting uglier."

"Listen."

"And soon you'll no longer be a person."

"The doughnut people have stopped attacking!"

I swallow, stop breathing, and just listen.

He's right. The doughnut people have stopped attacking the house.

"Maybe they got bored or found someone else to eat," I say.

I slather the remaining half of the first burrito in hot sauce. I raise the burrito to my mouth, letting hot sauce roll down my fingers before taking a bite. Whenever I eat a burrito without a side of tortilla chips, I let the hot sauce get all over my fingers, then between bites I suck on my fingers as if they are spicy popsicles.

There is the sound of a window breaking upstairs followed by a succession of thuds. We look at each other with mutual expressions of horror. The doughnut people have broken a window and are now inside the house.

I leap up from the couch and run into the kitchen, leaving the second burrito and the man with maple bars for toes behind.

But the man follows, screaming, "Holy fuck, what are we going to do?"

I grab the coconut halves off the counter on my way down to the basement. The man's toes clatter like hooves on the basement stairs.

We stand at the bottom of the staircase, light pouring in from the open doorway above.

"You forgot to shut the door, you fucking dipshit," I say.

"Sorry," he says.

I elbow him in the chest. "Well get up there and close it. What the hell is your problem?"

He's frozen.

I throw my elbow into his face and break his nose.

He scampers up the stairs, bleeding, reaching for the open door that lets in light.

Blood is always the thing that keeps us moving.

His fingers close around the door handle and in the same moment, a doughnut person appears in the gap, its gnarled head framed in fluorescent light.

The doughnut person bares frosted fangs.

The doughnut person sinks its fangs into the neck of the man with maple bars for toes.

The man with maple bars for toes punches the doughnut person in the face, and the doughnut person frowns, wiping custard blood from its nose.

The door is slammed shut and then barred. The man with maple bars for toes puts a hand over the hole in his neck and falls down the stairs.

I go over to him to check if he broke his neck in the fall.

I kneel beside him. I put a hand on his chest and feel nothing. I'm afraid to touch his neck because splintered bones are jutting out like the spiny fins of a tropical fish.

He totally broke his neck and I'm glad. It means he won't transform into a full-fledged doughnut person.

I look at his feet. He never put on his shoes like I told him to. His toes are maple bars, six inches long.

I realize I'm still clutching one half of the coconut in my right hand, while above, doughnut people make horrible gurgling sounds. And soon they will break down the door. And I'm trapped here with a person who is dead, and before that, I hated him. He murdered the girl I loved.

But at least I have this coconut.

I carve a happy face into the hard white meat of the coconut. I dig through the rind so light pours through the happy face. I put the coconut over my own face so I'm wearing it like a mask, because champions always die with a smile on.

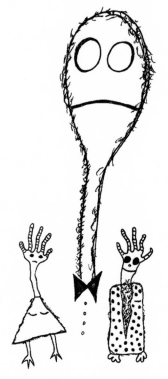

Free speech impassioned them.

THE PRISONERS

The correctional facility was made of pizza. It housed anorexic berserkers and the dripping of sauce and cheese was a constant torment to them.

The anorexic berserkers ate veal hamburgers for breakfast. They drank champagne for lunch. They stomached raw kimchee for dinner. They took burnt coffee with every meal.

One of the anorexic berserkers was a lumberjack. Another was a Dutch immigrant. Still another owned a gold mine. All were avid birdwatchers and free speech advocates.

One frigid winter, the correctional facility froze completely and caused a seven hour delay in the prisoners' schedule. They awoke seven hours late, ate veal hamburgers for breakfast seven hours late, searched for loopholes in anorexic law seven hours late, played board games seven hours late, etc.

In some places, the pizza walls of the correctional facility were still frozen. Among some prisoners, there circulated rumors that a miracle worker in the form of a crow would someday spring from the frozen parts, breaking wide a hole that led to the outside world, and freeing the anorexic berserkers at last.

Not a single anorexic berserker could say how long they had been imprisoned, or how long their sentence was supposed to carry on.

Despite the absence of windows and outdoor access, their avian interest held strong. The anorexic berserkers even slept and showered with their binoculars on, their water-logged Audubon guidebooks tucked neatly in the crooks of their sunken ribcages.

And how they loved free speech!

Free speech impassioned them.

They read the Russians to fill their hunger. They read the Greeks to forget the dripping of the walls. They fingered their own assholes when the dripping of the cheese and sauce became too much.

Wednesday was game night. They unanimously preferred Life over Monopoly, but they voted for Monopoly every Wednesday anyway. Since that mythic frigid winter, they tallied votes and started playing seven hours late. By then it was almost bedtime and they had to cut the game short, without a winner.

The prisoners dreamed of running, though they were too weak and frail to run. One among them owned a bunny. Whether it was the lumberjack or the Dutch immigrant, none could tell. The bunny may have changed hands nightly, or been no more than nasty rumor.

Over time, the correctional facility grew stale. The anorexic berserkers turned into gray skeletons and stopped living for hundreds of years at a time. Occasionally they got up and walked around, performing old rituals, still seven hours late. They never spoke except when prompted, and then only in guttural vowels that added up to nothing. Having lost their chance at freedom, speech meant nothing anymore.

They lived their dying days in a mountain of stinking cheese and molded sauce, and after crawling through so many centuries of rot, they were buried. But the anorexic berserkers kept on waiting for the miracle worker to save them from the ruined facility. Even though freedom meant nothing anymore, they watched for crows whenever they came alive, their binoculars wedged inside the pizza walls, seeing nothing but holding out hope anyway.

ANT FAT

Today I watched some ants eat a rotten nectarine.
The ants were obese,
like if you bit into their thoraxes
blubber would gush out instead of blood.

If I ever went on a rotten fruit diet
and walked around on six limbs all day,
if I remained fat despite so much effort,
I would just die of devastation,
maybe with a little ant fat on my lips,
warm and dripping from the kill.

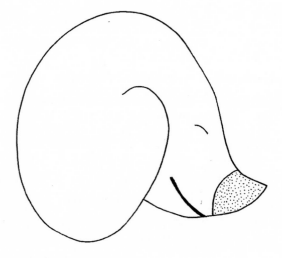

They dreamed collectively that night, and every night thereafter.

MOOP AND THE WOGGLE

Moop awoke to a flimsy knock on his cabin door. He opened the door to find some trout carrying a stream.

"Our stream grows sick wherever we put it down," said one. "Your garden, though, looks healthy, and we'd like to propose the following: let us stay, stream and all, and in return we are yours for the eating, if and when we're caught."

That is how Moop acquired a trout stream.

Soon there came birds, green snakes, praying mantises, ladybugs, spiders, cats, squirrels, deer, moose, goats, turtles, frogs, eels, and some creatures Moop could not identify. The garden produced enough fruit and vegetables for them all, and everyone was happy to contribute in whatever way they could: an industrious moose constructed a freshwater well; the insects formed a house band that played after dinner every night; the cats made dandelion wine; the goats opened a recycling plant. The sense of community was as bountiful and ever-present as sunlight.

The trouble started when the woggle moved in.

Moop never determined the lineage of the woggle, though he suspected more than one species had a paw in its blood. He found the woggle pleasant enough in conversation; most of the creatures found the woggle pleasant enough.

The trouble with the woggle concerned his food consumption.

After the third night with the woggle, the trout flopped out of the stream and knocked on Moop's door. "This isn't working," they said. "The woggle's eaten everything without a heartbeat."

Moop suggested brainstorming possible solutions and the trout agreed and threw around some ideas: kill the woggle; shoot the woggle; kill the woggle; eat the woggle, stew the woggle, barbecue the woggle; sell the woggle to the circus/knacker's yard/the Chinese pharmacy on 4th Street; kill the woggle; lock the woggle in the shed with the moose when horny; kill the woggle; eat the woggle; fry the woggle with onions; stew the woggle; skin the woggle; kill the woggle.

It was decided, finally agreed, that an eel should henceforth sleep coiled around the woggle's snout.

Miraculously, the next day yielded so much extra sunlight that the garden sprang up with new fruit and vegetables by late afternoon. The cats were irate because the woggle had drunk all the dandelion wine, and it would be several weeks until another batch was ready, but otherwise everyone was happy. They feasted and sang and told stories late into the night, and even allowed the woggle to eat more than its share.

When it was time for bed, the woggle donned its eel muzzle and everyone ambled off to their sleeping quarters. They dreamed collectively that night, and every night thereafter.

THE HONESTY OF MARSUPIALS IS A MARVELOUS THING

Marsupials are honestly marvelous.
Marvelously, marsupials are honest.
Honestly, marvelously, a marsupial.
Marsupials are marvelously honest.
Honesty is a marsupial marvel.

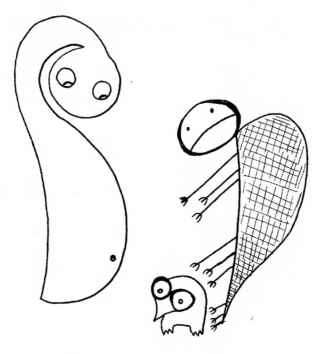

I will find you by your mountain face.

DEATH CARD

The game involved a deck of tarot cards and ancient, whittled checkers painted green and brown. Neither Tristan nor Emily knew how to play, but they sat at the foldout table in the empty sex shop and attempted to figure it out. Tristan had just pulled a death card when the old couple entered the shop. There was the tall, balding man and the short gray woman. Both of them dressed in identical red and white striped caps, red and white striped sweaters, blue jeans, and clunking brown shoes. Every Sunday, these Waldo impersonators came here like it was a cathedral of the Holy Ghost. The man paid Tristan for an hour in the private theater in back and the couple shuffled behind the moth-eaten velvet curtains demarcating the shop from the grunts and howls of orgasm and sodomy emanating from the disembodied static of the whirring, overheated projector.

Emily covered her mouth to keep her laughter from spilling out. Tristan stared at the velvet curtains with a nervous expression as he deposited the cash in the register. Red light reflected off the dust hanging in the air. Each orb of dust was a miniature lantern containing the wasted seed of a million lonely men brought together by flickering tits and prolapsed assholes. In the murk of these men, Emily appeared not alive – like a mannequin brought to motion by celluloid illusion. Tristan hated when she visited him at the shop for so many reasons, but she had to see with her own eyes all the freaks he told her about. The Waldo impersonators had been coming in for several months. He'd kept her out for that

23

long, but now she was here, and they were playing a game neither of them understood.

Tristan returned to the foldout table. Tightly, he held the death card between his thumb and index finger, like the lip of a flailing trout.

"Oh my god, that is so strange," Emily said. "What do they do in there?"

"Probably the same as everyone else. Watch the movie. Maybe get off."

"Do you think his penis has a little sweater too?" Emily asked with a devious smile.

"I don't know," Tristan said. This was the primary reason he hated Emily visiting him at work. She was so goddamn curious about everyone's business. She did not possess a dirty mind naturally, but she sometimes tried to talk dirty here. She succeeded, had a knack for it, and he wished it weren't so. People came here to cure, however temporarily, the mental and spiritual cramps that religion and booze could not touch. They came here not for the sweet staleness that clung to the air, but for an opportunity to reclaim the broken dreams signified by that odor.

"Tristan? Earth to Tristan? Hey, I'm talking to you."

His mind had wandered frequently in recent times, although it never wandered outward, only inward, as if he was sinking down into the mud of himself. This irritated Emily to no end, but he felt defenseless against the intermittent sinking.

She was doubly upset, he knew, because she called him by his name, a habit reserved for anger and lovemaking.

"If you're going to ignore me, I'll leave," she said.

"What, oh, sorry." He returned his eyes to the death card, now bent in half between his fingers.

"It's your turn," she said.

*

"Tonight's the night. You agreed to this, Tristan."

Applying beeswax lip balm, Tristan waffled in the doorway. He and Emily had made an agreement that when she got pregnant, he would dismantle his toy room to make space for the baby. The news arrived last week, but the floor to ceiling shelves holding his collection remained standing.

The doorbell rang and he retreated down the hall, welcoming the distraction.

The UPS guy had left a package on the doorstep.

"What is it?" Emily asked, standing behind him.

The package was from Grumble Toy, one of his favorite designers.

"This must be my Chubby Toughs," he said.

"Your what?"

"They're . . . cats."

He slit the packing tape with a key and removed six bubble-wrapped objects from the brown box.

"Want to open them with me?" he asked.

"Sure," she said, and began unwrapping one of the Chubby Toughs.

She enjoyed receiving mail and opening packages, so Tristan always tried to involve her in opening the toys he special ordered, even though she couldn't care less about the toys themselves.

"It looks like the Cheshire Cat with Down Syndrome," she said, inspecting the palm-sized white and purple cat.

She unwrapped another, this one orange and white, and made it attack the first while hissing between her teeth.

"Be careful, they're collectibles," Tristan said.

"How much did you spend on these?"

"About fifty dollars each, including shipping."

All six Chubby Toughs stood in a line between them. They were identical except in color.

"You spent three-hundred dollars on toy cats? We can't afford to throw money away like that."

"I got an unexpected royalty check from an old project. You

said I could spend surprise payments on whatever."

"That was before I got pregnant."

"I pre-ordered these months ago."

"Fine," she said. "You're still dismantling the toy room today."

"What are you going to do?"

"I've got to finish another Ferdinand and Fernando series. Some new hipster gallery in the southeast placed a big order."

"I'll get started on the toy room," Tristan said, saddened that his Chubby Toughs would never join the rest of his collection in his favorite room in the house.

"You can clear a place for them on the mantel if you want," Emily said. "They're cute."

As she went out to the garage, which had been converted into a crafts room since they owned no car, Tristan grumbled, "They're not cute. They're tough."

Their arrangement was simple, though perhaps a tad unconventional. Emily worked several days a week as an accountant for a local ice cream distributor. On the side, she sold her hand-sewn creatures to galleries, boutique shops, and on Etsy. Tristan worked in comics, mostly manga. He was the guy who converted the vertical Japanese speech bubbles to horizontal bubbles for the English editions, a thankless task for which he was unanimously hated by the writers, artists, and editors he worked with, but it was a necessary aspect of Japanese-to-English translations and everybody admitted that he did a better job than most. He also wrote for comics occasionally, although writing jobs were harder to come by. He'd been lucky to land a few gigs writing stories based on his favorite franchises – most notably *Aliens* and *Hellraiser* – but his contributions were never more than one-off stories in shoddy comics anthologies intended to cash in on popular properties. On weekends, he worked behind the counter at a friend's sex shop.

Pooling their various sources of revenue, Tristan and Emily had managed to put a down payment on a house in Portland's chic

Mississippi District, settled two miles north of the Willamette River. They managed to do this despite Tristan's toy obsession, which had cost them upward of fifteen grand to date.

His reign of toys ended with these cats, but in eight months their baby would be born and he could teach his child the joy and beauty of collecting, as his father had done for him nearly three decades before.

He placed the six Chubby Toughs on the mantel above the fireplace and said aloud what he imagined to be their mantra: "See all evil. Hear all evil. Speak all evil."

*

If the truth of a life always remained hidden from the one living it, why did he constantly feel as if he'd lived all this before?

That was the question troubling him as he turned on the record player, loud, and steeled himself for the agony of dismantling his plastic empire.

The record playing was *Song Force Crystal*, the latest from Hosannas, a melancholy noisepop band that consisted of two brothers. They were the Beach Boys by way of Joy Division, lost in some lovesick electric forest.

A mutual passion for sad music had initially brought Tristan and Emily together, and it was a passion that persisted. Happier than ever, they still loved their gloomy weather.

He decided to pack away his favorite toys first, beginning with Itchy Zoo, a mostly local collective of toy designers and pop surrealist street artists that maintained a miniature store inside a comic shop downtown. Even after all the toy exhibits he'd attended, after reading every book he could find on the vinyl toy revolution, not to mention countless hours browsing and researching toys online, Nomad the Gnome Man – the unofficial founder of Itchy Zoo – remained his all-time favorite artist.

Perhaps someday Tristan's collection would be worth a fortune, enough to pay their child's way through college, so that he or she might march straight into the screaming mouth of the real world without the crippling burden of debt.

*

By evening, the toys were all bubble-wrapped in cardboard boxes and the shelves were dismantled. He fetched Emily from the garage to show her the good work.

She sighed with satisfaction. "I honestly thought you'd chicken out."

"You owe me."

"Lucky for me I prepared to be surprised. Come here."

She took him by the hand and led him back out to the garage.

"You have two surprises," she said. "One is to reward your hard work, the other for your new collection."

"My new collection?"

She removed a fuzzy creature from a drawer and thrust it into his hands. The creature was an orange-skinned boy with a green dunce cap and a purple whale for a foot.

"Tetsuo," Tristan said, astonished, admiring this plush replica of his favorite vinyl figurine. He touched the small felt heart on Tetsuo's chest, the eyeless sockets in his face. "He looks just like the real toy."

"He looked lonely, so I made him a friend." From the same drawer, Emily removed a plush salmon riding a miniature wooden bicycle.

The bicycle appeared to have been carved by the same hand as the wooden Volkswagen Beetle that his father had given him, starting the toy craze. That Beetle was enshrined in a glass box in the living room. In fact, it had never been removed from the glass box, not once. His father gave him specific instructions to only break the glass in circumstances of extraordinary and dire need. For all the dire times Tristan had faced, none could be deemed extraordinary. Now here was a bicycle, free of all cages, free for this salmon to ride.

Tristan hugged Emily. He buried his face in her shoulder.

"Thank you so much," he said, close to tears.

"That's not all. Go look in the fridge."

Inside the house, he set Tetsuo and the cycling salmon on the kitchen table, then approached the fridge, where he discovered a pair of sealed mason jars filled with beer, which he suspected was Amnesia's Copacetic, one of the finest beers a city of great beer had to offer.

He began to reach for a jar, but Emily clucked disapprovingly.

"If I'm going to swell with your demon spawn, I want to get in my fill of bike rides first."

"Where do you want to ride?"

"Across the river to Powell's."

"Can we stop in at Itchy Zoo?" Tristan asked, but then remembered that his collecting days were over. "Oh, never mind." Besides, it was a Sunday evening. They would be closed.

"We can go to Sizzle Pie for dinner. How's that?"

"Fair enough."

And so they embarked on a quest for baby books and artisan punk rock pizza, traveling by the mode of transportation preferred by plush salmon.

*

The lights of Broadway Bridge glimmered on the dark water of the Willamette, and a warm summer breeze blew in from nowhere like the ghost of last winter's warmest fire. Tristan and Emily crossed the bridge on their matching red single speed bikes.

Out of habit, Tristan veered down Broadway and turned right on Couch, passing Floating World Comics and Itchy Zoo. He felt lust for the toys inside, chased by sadness, knowing he would never have them.

"Itchy Zoo is hosting a new show you'd like," he said, as they rode side by side.

"I'm sure they are."

"Stegoforest. It's stegosauruses with trees growing out of their backs."

"A new toy line?"

"They're more like sculptures."

"Ah, yes. Sculptures," Emily said sarcastically.

"What's wrong with that?"

"Nothing."

"No, I want to know."

"Just forget it."

Emily had always resented his toy collection. He suspected that she was jealous and even hurt that he spent so much time obsessing over creations that were not her own. She made creatures too. He loved her creatures. His heart had simply chosen vinyl a long time ago.

They locked their bikes outside the main entrance on Burnside and entered Powell's.

"I'm going to look at baby books. Where are you going to be?" Emily asked.

"I'll be in the café."

"Reading *Gantz*, I suspect?"

"Affirmative, Captain," he said in his best Spock voice.

"Come find me in a while. You don't have to browse with me, but I need you to cull the herd."

They kissed and exchanged loving pet names before parting. Tristan passed through the blue room without paying much attention. He paused in the entrance of the gold room to eye the new science fiction and fantasy releases before continuing on to the corner window section, where one found superhero comics, erotica, nautical fiction, and manga.

The next volume of *Gantz* was plastic-sealed to prevent minors from reading it. He discretely tore away the plastic before moving into the café.

He sat alone in a street-facing chair. Outside, two homeless men were engaged in an argument.

"Don't touch my fuckin' shit, man," shouted the one wearing a yellow poncho.

The other homeless guy, bald and wearing a FUCK CHRISTMAS, FUCK YOU t-shirt, reached out to touch a bucket held by Yellow Poncho.

"I said don't touch my shit."

Apparently fed up, Yellow Poncho overturned the bucket on Fuck You's head, drenching him in water and miniature great white sharks. The bucket had been filled with sharks.

Tristan leaned forward to watch the sharks flop on the sidewalk. He counted a dozen.

"Teach you a lesson, bitch," spat Yellow Poncho, and stormed off.

Fuck You bent over and plucked a shark off the sidewalk. He grinned at Tristan as he slid the shark down his throat.

Tristan scooted his chair backward in confusion and horror. The chair screeched against the tile floor and people turned to look at him.

Tristan went to find Emily in the baby section, leaving *Gantz* behind.

*

Hiroya Oku, the writer and illustrator of *Gantz*, had pioneered a technique to suggest motion in visual storytelling. He utilized his breakthrough to represent the jiggling of breasts. Like the Japanese scientist who harvested the energy of an electric eel to light up a Christmas tree, Oku's genius was wasted on the ephemeral. Great thinkers of the past dreamed of God and immortality. Now they dreamed of manga breasts and eel-powered Christmas trees that could be seen from outer space.

Tristan saw beauty in this new world. He believed that beneath the surface of such artistic and scientific detritus existed truths far more real and hard and polished than God and immortality. This belief, however, was not the reason he read *Gantz*. The '*Tron* by way of Sartre's *No Exit*' storyline had never appealed to him. Less so did the seething, gratuitous sexuality. He read *Gantz* because it contained excellent speech bubbles.

The majority of Tristan's innermost ruminations concerned speech bubbles. This was the case long before he began working on manga translations. If it wasn't for speech bubbles, he would have never picked up comics, American or otherwise, at all. Prose fiction and film were both more evolved, more dynamic, but they lacked what he loved most, which were speech bubbles. He collected vinyl figures because nothing came closer to the texture of speech bubbles, the way they felt when he touched them in dreams. That was why Emily's creatures, as much as he loved them, would never penetrate the core of his being, and why, at his very best, he would never amount to more than a master of the trivial.

At least, in a city like Portland, with a loving, supportive wife like Emily, he could embrace his own insignificance with a relative amount of ease. In Portland, he could even be deluded into believing that his work was somehow important.

He would make a good father, though. Of that he was certain.

*

"I know this guide for hip parents looks stupid, but it has some neat information you don't get in other books."

They were sitting in Sizzle Pie, waiting for their order. Tristan flipped through the stack of baby books Emily had bought while she explained the pros and cons of each book. When they went on these excursions to Powell's, he usually selected the baby books most appealing to him from a large stack of potential candidates. Tonight, he'd been so disturbed by the shark incident that he told her to buy all the books she'd grabbed. She took it as a gesture of goodwill and, not wanting to reveal the selfish motives for his kindness, Tristan refrained from describing what he'd witnessed. Something about the occurrence had instilled in him an urgent desire to leave the bookstore despite the fact the homeless guys were outside and not in the store.

Perhaps he was experiencing toy withdrawal.

"This one seems good," he said, referring to a guidebook on infant-friendly hikes and campsites in the Pacific Northwest.

"I knew you'd be happy about that one. We didn't want to miss out on nature, and we won't have to. Oh, this one is good too." She put the camping book aside in favor of a book about BDSM for pregnant women.

Tristan grinned. "We really won't have to go without."

"Yeah, who knew pregnancy would spice up our sex life."

"If there's a hole, there's a way."

"Don't be gross."

"I was just saying."

"I know. Don't."

Their order was called and Tristan went to the counter to retrieve it, collecting nutritional yeast and crushed red pepper from the condiments tray on his return.

He'd ordered a slice of the Vegan Angel of Doom, which was topped with fake mozzarella, jalapenos, pineapple, shaved almonds, and cilantro. She'd ordered the Slaughter of the Soil, a simple slice boasting spinach, tomato, and artichoke hearts.

He poured too much yeast and red pepper on his pizza, again, for which she rightfully chided him, but afterward she laughed and said, "I love you."

"Aardvark Sauce is the best," she said, even though she was not currently, nor had she ever, eaten pizza with Aardvark Sauce.

"Yeah, Aardvark Sauce is pretty good. Pretty damn good," he said. "We should get a bottle for home."

Sometimes love was as simple as agreeing that Aardvark Sauce was good and not letting it go any further.

They finished their pizza and fled gently into the night.

*

When they returned home, Emily found several urgent messages from her father on the answering machine.

Tristan sat at the kitchen table, sipping Copacetic from a mason jar, as Emily listened to her father.

Tears welled up in her eyes. She was gibbering nonsense by the time she hung up the phone.

Tristan seated her at the table. After several minutes, she calmed down enough to break the news.

"Charlotte was in an accident. They helicoptered her to ICU in Spokane."

"Wait, hold on. An accident?"

"Another driver saw her car veer off the road. They think it was intentional but maybe not. Maybe she fell asleep."

"Where's your dad? Is he home?"

"No, he's halfway to Spokane. He called me from the road." She bolted up and stormed toward the bedroom. "Oh, shit. I have to pack."

Tristan followed her down the hallway. "Pack for what?"

"I'm going to see my sister."

"How?"

"Can you get online and check Priceline while I pack? Find the earliest flight to Spokane in the morning."

"How are we going to afford that?"

Emily's face turned splotchy. Her eyes swelled with rage. "How are we going to pay for that, Tristan? Why don't we start by selling those fucking cats? I could have made cats just like that for you, but while you're fawning over every new hunk of plastic, where's the shit I slaved over for you?"

"I don't know what you're talking about," he said with a blank expression on his face.

"Because you left them on the floor. That's how much you care about the things I make you."

"You know that's not true."

"Then fucking prove it."

"I'll go book your flight."

"Don't bother."

Tristan retreated. He paused to pick up the plush imitation Tetsuo and the salmon cyclist from beneath the kitchen table. He set them on the table and continued on to the living room. He logged onto the desktop computer, opened Firefox, and typed 'priceline' into the search engine.

He wondered if Emily needed a hotel room. She and her father would probably stay in the hospital until Charlotte's condition stabilized. If they needed a hotel, they could figure that out when the time came. He searched for Flights Only from Portland to Spokane and waited for Priceline Shatner to negotiate the best deals.

He selected a flight departing at six in the morning. Emily's return plans were unknown. He decided to leave that up to her, to be determined at a later date, as well.

He submitted the order, printed her itinerary, and took it to the bedroom, setting it atop the blue suitcase on the unmade bed, where Emily lay curled like a wounded cat.

"Your flight leaves at six."

"Thank you. I'm sorry for being so horrible."

"It's okay."

"Do you really hate my creatures that much?"

"Honey, I love your creatures."

"Then why don't you act like it?"

"What kind of reaction are you looking for?"

"You don't express yourself."

"I was nearly crying when you gave those creatures to me."

"*Nearly* is the key. You were *nearly* crying, which means nothing."

"How's your sister?"

"Probably dead."

"She'll survive. She's tough."

"Please don't talk about her. I can't bear to think about her lying comatose when I can't be there beside her."

"Sorry."

Emily sat up on her haunches. "Hey, can I show you something I've never shown anyone?"

"Sure."

"You have to promise to keep it a secret."

"I promise."

Emily made a face unlike any Tristan had seen her make before. Her expression was not sad or happy, but somehow vegetal, he supposed.

"What's that?" he asked.

"It's my mountain face. In our next lives, I will be a mountain. That's the face I'll be making for all time, until you find me, at least."

"I will find you by your mountain face."

"Will you love me when I'm a mountain?"

"Geologically, yes."

"I look forward to that time," she said.

White glaciers split the crumbling edifice of her mountain face until, if you looked at her with the sound on mute or in a photograph, you would swear she was screaming.

Tristan moved in for an embrace.

They proceeded to strip each other down, first pants and shirts, followed by flesh and organs and eyes, until they lay as bone on bone, in yellow dust, petrifying.

THREE PEOPLE LOSE THEIR GENITALS WHILE GETTING NAKED

It is good to stand with a person standing behind your back
to use their arms as your arms
to unzip your pants
as a person standing in front of you
uses your arms as their arms
to unzip their pants
and the person in back rips off the arms
of the person in front
and uses the severed arms as their own severed arms
to unzip their pants.
The wind sucks three pairs of genitals
out of three pairs of unzipped pants
and blows the genitals into a tree.
Now your genitals are stuck in a tree
and the person in front of you is bleeding on your shirt.
It is good to stand with a person standing behind your back
to use their arms as your arms
to unbutton your shirt.

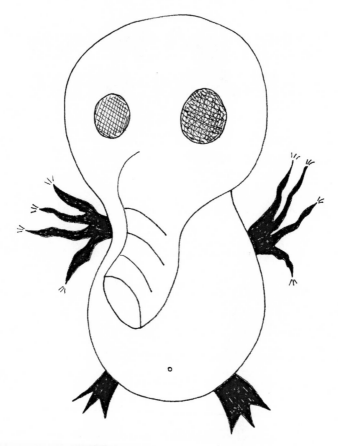

Filled with the magical flying cat,
Leviathan floats toward the open window.

A BIRTHDAY IN HELL

Leviathan and Lilith are having a joint birthday party and I am all alone, waiting for them to open their gifts. Nobody likes Leviathan and Lilith enough to spend a lot of money on them. I don't even like them enough and I spent a lot of money, but I'm in the business of buying friendship.

I go into the kitchen for another free beer. I feel disappointed when I go someplace and there's no free alcohol. Like the dentist's office or the DMV.

Some demons think I'm a failure because I can't pass the driving test. That's what it takes to be someone in Hell. You've got to own the road. It doesn't matter that I'm royalty.

I grab two cans of PBR from the case in the refrigerator. I stick one of the cans in my coat pocket. I make a display of pocketing it so the two demons talking in the kitchen know exactly what I'm doing.

That I'm stealing beer from those who are offering it for free.

And one of the demons, the female, gives me a dirty look.

The other demon, the male, is too busy hitting on the female and drinking free beer to care about me.

My theft defeats his theft because I have no need for what I've taken.

I return to the living room and chest bump someone who isn't there. I am excellent at faking good times.

Everyone is in love with exactly one other demon at this birthday party.

Leviathan sees me standing alone. He smiles and nods, letting me know that he's happy I showed up, but also that he's not interested in talking to me.

I nod and smile so he knows I feel the same.

He turns away, giving me a view of the tiny insect wings that sag like wet dishrags from his monstrous hunchback.

I'm a prince of moderate importance, but unpopular.

I walk across the living room to the free snack tray. There are chips and guacamole, peanuts and peanut M&Ms.

I consider pulling Leviathan or Lilith aside and solemnly informing them that I am allergic to peanuts and must go at once.

They will say, "Don't eat the peanuts."

I will say, "It's spiritual."

I stick a finger in the guacamole then lower my head and walk toward the bathroom, my finger curled into a hook.

I lock myself in the bathroom to wait for gift-opening time.

I pour my beer out in the sink. I look at myself in the mirror while the beer drains out of the can. I raise my guacamole hook finger above my head. I stab myself in the chest, smearing guacamole on the front of my goatskin shirt.

"The man with the green hook will kill himself anytime," I say.

I crumple the empty beer can and toss it in the bathtub.

I lower the toilet lid and sit down on the toilet.

There's a litter box across from the toilet.

And tonight I'm such a jokester.

I stand up and pull down my pants. I squat over the litter box. Eventually a big shit comes out.

I rake litter over the shit.

Leviathan and Lilith will be so surprised when they see this big shit their cat took.

They will stop feeding it crappy food. From now on, their cat will only eat dictators, traitors, and all the worst sinners.

Because I took a shit in the litter box.

Because I am a saint of cats, holy in all conceivable ways.

As an afterthought, I take the PBR out of my pocket and hide it in the tampon box beneath the sink because some flows are heavier than others.

I decide to return to the living room. I cannot stay in the bathroom when it smells this bad.

Lilith sits on the couch, laughing, touching the knee of a bearded skinny guy in a cardigan sweater. In some circles of Hell, it's fashionable to invite humans down for birthday parties. I really hate that.

I make eye contact with Lilith. My eyes say that it is not the time to be touching the knees of bearded skinny guys.

Lilith gets up from the couch and comes over to me.

"What is it?" she says.

"I think it's the peanuts," I say.

"What?"

"I'll tell you in the kitchen."

We go into the kitchen.

"Is something the matter?" she says, pulling two beers out of the refrigerator. She hands one of them to me.

"Your cat." I open the beer and take a long gulp, as if I need to brace myself for what's about to be said.

"What about my cat?" she says, frowning.

"I think maybe it ate some peanuts. I hear they're not good for cats and, like, there's this shit in the litter box that's unreal. I don't know your cat or its bathroom habits, but that shit seems abnormal. You'd better check it out."

This is the part where I'm supposed to say *just kidding*, but the look on her face breaks my heart.

"Our cat is dead," she says.

Oh, fuck.

She rushes out of the kitchen before I can say anything. I consider leaving the party right now, slipping out of the apartment and returning to my own place, three fiery layers below this one. I don't want to see that face again. I don't want to be asked to explain myself.

Whenever I see horrible faces, I'm somehow always the cause of them. Whenever the faces ask me to explain myself, the wrong words come out. The wrong words and a lot of pointless apologies.

Lilith's shrieks quiet the partygoers.

I leave the kitchen and make a beeline for the front door.

The female demon from the kitchen steps in front of me, battleaxe raised above her head. "I knew he was up to no good," she says to the male demon, who stands beside her, ogling her metal-plated breasts.

"What is it, Lil?" Leviathan says, reclining in a leather chair as two scaly vixens stroke his blubbery tail.

The obese whale's mouth is full of peanut M&Ms. Flakes of candy-coating adorn his mouth like the glittery lip gloss of pre-teen girls. He washes down the M&Ms with an entire can of beer.

"That asshole shit in Spooky's litter box," Lilith calls from the bathroom.

"Which asshole?" Leviathan says. He fishes between his gray folds of belly fat and removes another PBR. He shoves the entire can into his gaping maw without bothering to pop the tab. The can bursts in his mouth, but he doesn't mind. He gnashes the aluminum into pencil shavings.

The demons in the room shift their eyes nervously, accusingly. The bearded skinny guy looks scared shitless, but so do I. That's part of Hell's punishment. When you're a demon, you cannot hide your guilt.

All eyes fix on me.

I point at the bearded skinny guy, hoping the beer has put the others in the mood for torturing an innocent. "It was him," I say. "That's the asshole. I saw him do it."

Lilith emerges from the bathroom, her eyes glowing red, her spade tail poised, ready to strike.

"You're telling me you watched this human shit in the litter box?" she says.

I lower my chin to the guacamole stain on my chest. I'm not

strong enough to lie so blatantly to Lilith. She's the only one who holds that kind of power over me. But if I tell the truth, she'll dice me up and serve me as birthday cake.

"Answer me," she says, cracking her tail.

I give my best fake laugh and clap my hands, acting as if this is all a joke, which it is. Or was. "Oh, Lilith, you really had me going there. Hey Leviathan, you and Lilith should open your presents now. I got you something really special and if you hold off any longer, I won't be here when you open it. I told Cerberus I'd cover his guard duty tonight."

"As if Cerberus would trust you," somebody mutters.

"You're just jealous because you brought a lame gift and I got them something awesome. Come on, Levi, let's do present time."

"Cake and presents," the whale says, nodding.

"That's right, cake and presents," I say, glancing over at Lilith. She's beyond pissed.

I find my gift in the stack of presents and bring it to Leviathan before anyone can stop me. "Here you go," I tell him, laying the box wrapped in human skin on his bulbous stomach.

"Thanks," he says, squirming in his chair. He's obviously uncomfortable about the tension in the room, but too excited to resist the gift.

And yes, I am a champion of others' weaknesses.

Leviathan starts to tear away the wrapping, then hesitates. He looks to Lilith. "Aren't you going to help?" he says.

"Fine," she says, crossing the room. "It had better be good."

Together, they unwrap the box. Lilith strokes the skin wrapping, impressed by its quality. Leviathan licks his lips, hoping the gift is edible. I inch my way toward the door, in case they're disappointed.

The box is made of obsidian but as thin as a tissue. It falls apart in the whale's clumsy hands, revealing the gift within.

Everyone in the room gasps. For a bunch of demons, they're weak-willed pansies. I've known humans more cruel and insensitive.

"Don't you love it?" I say.

"It's our cat," Lilith says. "You murdered our fucking cat and wrapped him in a box."

"Oh no," I say, holding my hands up, shaking my head in protest. "I paid a lot of money for that thing. It's not your cat, Lilith. It's a magical flying cat, and it's not dead. It's just sleeping. To wake it up, we've got to baste it in saliva. I'll run into the kitchen and grab a pot for everyone to spit in. We can wake the kitty up right now."

Lilith lunges for me. She drags me to the ground, punching me and raking her claws across my face as her tail coils in preparation for a knockout strike.

Demons crowd around us, egging her on.

"Leviathan, no!" somebody shouts.

Lilith hesitates. I squirm out from under her and crawl toward the kitchen, expecting her to pounce on me, but when I turn back, she's looking at the bearded skinny guy. He's the one who shouted. He shouts again. "Somebody help, stop Leviathan!"

Leviathan is eating the cat.

Everyone in the room converges on the obese whale in the recliner. Lilith starts doing the Heimlich on him.

"That's not going to work unless he's actually choking on the cat," says the female demon with the axe. "Let me decapitate him."

"Decapitation won't solve the problem either," her male companion says, "not if he swallows the cat before you cut off his head."

"Everyone, be quiet!" Lilith says.

I stand in the back of the crowd, wondering if I should beat an exit while I still can. I decide to stick around.

The cat's hind legs and tail vanish as Leviathan gulps it down. Lilith starts to cry. The bearded skinny guy rushes over to comfort her. A few demons turn away. Everyone is sad about the cat.

I start to tiptoe out of the room, before their grief turns to anger, but a mewling halts me in my hoof tracks. There is another mewling, then another, coming from Leviathan's belly.

The cat is alive.

"Quick, open a window," I say, hoping it's not too late to redeem myself.

When nobody jumps into action, I run to the largest window and throw it open. The mewling inside Leviathan grows louder as he floats out of the leather recliner like a balloon. His tiny insect wings are flapping, but his wings are not the reason he's floating.

Filled with the magical flying cat, Leviathan floats toward the open window. He's too scared or surprised to say anything. He hasn't flown in years. He used to love flying!

Leviathan gets stuck in the window frame, so I call on the other demons to help me push him out. The female demon sets down her axe and lines up beside me, pushing with all her might. Even Lilith and the bearded skinny guy help out.

When Leviathan is freed, he soars out of the apartment, above the highways gridlocked with rush hour traffic, and along the River Styx. Soon, he is just a little gray dot, indistinguishable from all the other dots that could be pterodactyls, dragons, or other flying whales. Soon, the river will spill into an ocean of blood, and Leviathan will go down, returning to the place where he always belonged.

"Happy birthday," I say, hoping that after all these years in Hell, someone finally counts me as one of their friends.

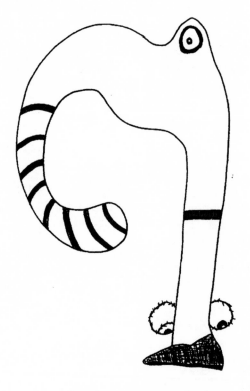

Pity the country was dead.
Pity he wasn't famous.

BRIEF HISTORY OF AN AMPUTEE

I. On Animals

He found his mom's Def Leppard tapes when he was five. His stepfather whipped her with a belt when he heard what the amputee, not an amputee at the time, was listening to. The night his stepfather whipped his mom, the boy had a dream about a deaf leopard. The leopard communicated telepathically. She told him the best use of anyone's time was to stab a knife into his face, and then she tried to eat him.

II. Portrait of the Amputee as a Young Man

When he was fifteen, they sent him away to Vista Del Mar, a youth mental facility in southern California. He'd been put on pills by the family doctor several months before, but the pills set him off even worse. The doctor prescribed Zyprexa for schizophrenia and/ or bipolar disorder and Wellbutrin for depression. In Vista Del Mar they excused Wellbutrin from his diet and fed him protein shakes because he was losing weight.

He met decent but troubled people. An overweight Hispanic lesbian claimed to be a Wiccan and a Satanist. He set her straight on her religion. Bobby was sixteen. He had a Jack Skellington tattoo. He was in Vista for shooting at someone.

Nobody received help, and even though the doctors were concerned about his weight, they never gave him the egg salad sandwich he was told he had to eat in addition to the bland, unhealthy meals they fed them. Kids in there were losing weight.

He only stayed for a few days. He begged his parents to get him out. Nobody got help in Vista Del Mar. You waited and waited and waited for something to pass that never would. They made the males and females switch dorms twice, for no real purpose that anyone saw. Even the doctors admitted the futility of the place. Most people watched television. The boy read Lovecraft, Eliot, and Plath.

He had seen a demon in the summer prior to this winter visit. That's why they sent him there. He was depressed, he knew, but not unsound. The demon was gray and eyeless. It stood over him one night. He had experienced ghosts in his childhood as well.

He was straight edge, drug free, so it most certainly was not drugs.

He took Zyprexa until June, when he began slipping the pill under his tongue when his parents gave it to him each night. By the end of summer, he thought he needed to burn down the church where he was baptized as a baby in order to free himself.

Free himself from what, he'll never know.

He remembers that summer, lying on his bed and feeling up a girl who was three years older. They'd met online. She had big tits, but she wouldn't let him fuck her. They never spoke again after that.

He hid away and wrote and played guitar. He lost his boyish charm. He grew ugly and fat. He wrote a song a day for several years. He sold tapes of his songs that he recorded in his parents' basement. This period was characterized by intense focus on his work, fueled in part by insomnia. Never sleep. Even when he drifted off while driving and flipped his car on Highway 41, he still couldn't sleep. He still can't. He won't.

After high school he moved to the beach and fell into his most manic phase. He believed shadowy agents were coming for him. He failed to sleep thirty-odd nights in a three month period. He wrote and recorded up to seven songs a day. He fell in love for the first time in his life. He will not talk about her. When she refused him, he decided to see some of the world and bought a one-way ticket to South America

He was innocent. He was not this angry, violent person you see today. He had damaged many people, but it was nothing compared to the things he'd done to the woman in the House of Agonies. It was nothing like the past few years, the past few days, or the past few hours, but right now he is learning how to open up about the better times.

III. How the Amputee Became an Amputee While in South America

When the witch doctor amputated his legs, it became clear to the man that his diabetes had gotten out of hand. He had lost his entire penicillin supply on his third day in the jungle, when a giant river fish overturned his boat. The fish was insane, Stromboni, his guide, told him later. After decades of toxic runoff from America-owned factories, a parasitic worm had appeared in the river. The worm lived in the brains of river animals. It gave them a taste for human flesh. The river incident happened weeks ago. Now Stromboni was dead.

Until the amputation, the man had forgotten all about the giant fish. He'd seen much worse in the days that followed. He had crossed alligator nesting grounds and outwitted a clouded leopard god. He had fallen in love all over again. He had grown sick.

The witch doctor cauterized his leg stump with the viscous sap of a tree that only grew underground. The sap healed wounds as well as any first world sterilizer, but it burned like hell. The man bit down on the leathery root in his mouth. He buried his overgrown fingernails into the calloused meat of his palms and fought against the ropes that fastened his limbs to the hut's dirt floor.

The root was removed and a wooden bowl was pushed against his lips. He was forced to drink. The liquid solidified in his mouth. He tried to spit it out, but already his lips were fastened shut. The witch doctor lay a hand on his forehead and told him to breathe. He took a breath, somehow, and another breath.

"You need no words to breathe," the witch doctor said. "You need air. The cactus mud is full of air. Swallow it and you may breathe in the river."

IV. The Last Song the Amputee Ever Wrote Before Setting Fire to His Guitar and Flying Back to America, Only to Discover a Dead, Deserted Country (Despite the Empty Airports, There Were Thousands of Commercial Planes in the Sky), So He Wandered Legless Until He Came to the House of Agonies

He drops his pants and falls on hands and knees.
He sheds a tear and bites his tongue, nose against the floor.
His father says, "I'm sorry son. I'm sorry for what it's worth.
Forgive me for my duty. In punishment is truth."
The belt cracks down against his back. He feels its leather girth.
"You are strong for you are my son, but what you did was wrong."
The belt cracks down against his back. He tastes its leather tongue.
He sees his brother wave from the boat upon the pond.
His father says, "I could never bear to lose you."
He sees the boat keel over. His brother, he goes down.
The belt cracks down against his back. He is warmed by his own blood.
His father says, "I will never let you freeze."

The belt cracks down, the belt cracks down, the belt cracks down once more.

His father says, "It purifies your blood."

He sees his brother's face when they dragged him up on shore.

Someone says, "I'm sorry, for what it's worth."

V. Cult Discography

While the amputee was in South America, before he became the amputee, he picked up a cult following. His home-recorded tapes became rare collector's items. He'd deleted his MySpace music page prior to leaving the country, so nobody knew who he was for a while. People speculated on blogs and message boards.

The amputee had omitted contact information from the liner notes of his recordings. This, it should be noted, was a totally accidental oversight. He honestly did not set out to be 'mysterious' about himself. He'd just never considered the possibility that someone might enjoy his music enough to try and seek him out. He wrote and recorded music, leaving the tapes in public places and sometimes giving them away to people on the street, because he felt driven by an inward light. The same light led him to South America and, eventually, to the House of Agonies.

He played one live show in his whole career, opening for the punk band Total Chaos at Jerry's Pizza when he was seventeen. They booed him offstage. This was before Against Me! and folk punk. Anarchists did not appreciate acoustic music in those days.

No more than a few dozen copies were known to exist of any of his recordings. Pitchfork got wind of this whole thing when a purportedly one-of-a-kind tape called NOTHING BUT SKIN AND TEETH sold on eBay for $639.23. By this point, most of the amputee's known discography was available for illegal download, but nobody had heard NOTHING BUT SKIN AND TEETH.

Pitchfork compared him unfavorably to Jandek and David

Tibet. The reviewer expressed some doubt over the validity of the Skin and Teeth Auction, as she coined it (the Pitchfork reviewer was a female).

A few months later, the internet disappeared. All record of the amputee's cult status was erased completely.

He returned, legless, from South America shortly after.

Pity the country was dead.

Pity he wasn't famous.

VI. The Woman

He found the woman in the gutter. He took her to his room and he tied her up and raped her.

The leopard and the platypus took little interest in the woman. They had been living in the House of Agonies when the amputee moved in. The only thing they asked after he found the woman was that he pay a little more rent. Right from the start, the amputee loved the woman, so he agreed to pay more rent.

He fucked her and loved her and paid higher rent to keep her. He drew her face on the floorboards, drawing her over and over so the faces blurred and the amputee broke down sobbing. He stabbed himself in the wrist with a pencil. The lead tip broke off within.

More than anything, he wanted her to love him.

But he didn't know how.

The amputee didn't know how to convince the woman to love him.

If only she could see her face on the floorboards, the black lump in his wrist.

The amputee talked to her about tropical islands. He asked if she would like to go on a vacation.

Sometimes he stared into her eyeless socket for hours.

This one-eyed woman, she was everything to the amputee. He

had to keep her tied up. He couldn't let her get away.

VII. The Worry of His Domain

The worry of his domain swelled into a thing that could sit next to him and breathe. Dragging himself along by his hands, the worry followed. He rolled down the streets, swinging a deflated balloon like a limp dog as the worry galloped behind and nipped at his stumps. Not himself these days. On other days perhaps, there was the hope or possibility of returning to his former self, but no more than a glimmer. Now he was departing the House of Agonies, gone into a place where all the roads were made of sand, converging. He would have a final showdown with his worry. Only one of them would return to the House of Agonies that evening. He wondered how easy it would be to stab a knife into something you could always feel but never touch. He wondered, if the worry returned in his place, would the woman notice?

Where's the narwhals at?

NARWHALS

A cowboy was leaning against the wall outside Fred Meyer, smoking a cigarette. He said howdy to me and I complimented him on his cowhide vest.

I went into the store and looked at what was new in the video rental machine. They were featuring a horror movie about a killer eyeball and a family comedy about a police dog that dies and comes back from the afterlife to fight crime as a ghost. The family comedy was called *Ghost Police Dog II*, so I guess it was a sequel or something.

Red apples were on sale but I didn't want any red apples.

The organic bananas looked rotten.

On my way to the beer aisle, I got stuck behind an obese woman in a motorized wheelchair. She'd stopped in front of an end freezer full of vegetarian fake meat products, like meatless corndogs and meatless orange chicken. They came in green packages so consumers knew they were doing something responsible and good for the earth by purchasing them.

The obese woman's fat hung over the sides of her wheelchair like the foamy head of a beer flowing over the lip of a pint glass in slow motion.

I waited for her to move and when she didn't move, I listened to what she was saying. She was repeating the same line again and again.

"Where's the narwhals at? Where's the narwhals at?"

She coughed a lot too.

In the basket of her motorized wheelchair sat a leaky wine box and a large soft drink cup from Taco Bell. The lid was off and purple liquid sloshed around on the inside.

This woman was drunk and just wanted some narwhals to eat.

She wanted to eat some vegetarian narwhals, if at all possible.

She wanted to be responsible.

She continued saying, "Where's the narwhals at?" for as long as I stood there. I had to walk around the hot fried chicken stand to move past her.

I got a six pack of the cheapest IPA and some generic cereal that contained marshmallows shaped like sea creatures.

The obese woman was still muttering to herself when I passed her on my way to the self-checkout stands.

"Where's the narwhals at? Where's the narwhals at?"

I thought about reaching into the freezer and pulling out some random green packages and stacking them on her box of wine and saying, "Here's the narwhals." I thought about telling security that she was drinking in the store just so I could watch them attempt to kick her out and/or arrest her. I thought about how people get desperate for things that don't exist.

After I paid for my beer and cereal, I went to one of the Red Box machines and tried to rent *Ghost Police Dog II* and the horror movie about the killer eyeball, but both of them were checked out. None of the other movies available sounded good to me, so I left the store.

On my way out I saw the cowboy, galloping up Burnside on a white horse, heading toward the dark west hills. And right then I saw my death fifty years in the future, and I knew everything was going to be just fine.

DEAD SUPERMODELS

You never know
when Thurston Moore
might show you his balls.

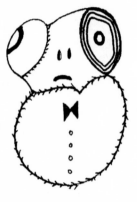

And going to the mall is a wonderful thing.

PABLO RIVIERA, DEPRESSED, OVERWEIGHT, AGE 31, GOES TO THE MALL

Pablo Riviera goes to the mall and buys a pair of bunny slippers, a serious drama film about a serious historical event, and two dozen miniature sugar cookies from his favorite cookie shop. These are the necessary supplies for a good Saturday night.

Pablo goes to the food court and feels overwhelmed. There are so many choices. How can he possibly choose what to eat? The mall contains some of the best restaurants in the world. There is almost too much great food, he decides. Almost too much.

Pablo makes a compromise. Since he feels guilty about choosing any one restaurant over all the others, he selects a single item from several of his favorites. He orders a corndog from Hot Dog on a Stick, a taco from Taco Bell, a Happy Meal from McDonalds, and a smoothie from Orange Julius.

He is overweight and concerned that eating so much food will cause him to gain more weight, but shopping makes him hungry. Between the parking lot, the slipper store, the movie store, the cookie shop, and the food court, he figures he has walked at least a quarter mile. And he will walk another quarter mile on his return. When Pablo realizes he will walk half a mile today, he feels a sense of accomplishment. If only he came to the mall every day, he would be healthy, but it takes a lot of work to go to the mall. A lot of hard work. He has to drive there, for one. And muster up the social energy to talk to all those cashiers.

Pablo walks around the food court, collecting his food. He sits at the table closest to the steak sandwich place because the steak sandwich place smells the best. Unfortunately, their steak sandwiches are not as good as Arby's. That is the one thing wrong with the mall's food court. There is no Arby's.

Pablo thinks maybe he should order a steak sandwich anyway. He has only tried the steak sandwiches three or four times. He doesn't like their steak sandwiches, but wants to give them a fair chance. Pablo is the most patient, understanding person he knows.

He gets up and orders a steak sandwich and chili cheese fries.

He sits back down and takes a sip of his smoothie. It's probably the best smoothie he has ever had. He unwraps the taco, slides the corndog off the stick, and shoves the corndog into the taco. Corndog tacos are Pablo's favorite food ever. He is surprised Taco Bell and Hot Dog on a Stick have not formed a joint partnership to sell corndog tacos despite the many customer feedback forms he has filled out insisting they do just that.

The first bite of the corndog taco is majestic. The second bite is transcendental.

Pablo doesn't put hot sauce or ketchup on his food. He thinks condiments ruin the flavor.

When half the corndog taco is gone, he looks down at the Happy Meal box sitting before him. The Happy Meal looks lonely.

"I'm sorry, Happy Meal," he whispers.

He opens the Happy Meal box and takes out the cheeseburger. He feels despondent. Something must be wrong. Did he buy the right slippers? The right movie? He removes the Happy Meal toy from the box. "Oh, that's the problem," he says.

The toy is a Transformers action figure that he already owns. He smiles. His unconscious mind is very clever. He was feeling bad because he received a duplicate toy. His brain knew what toy was in the Happy Meal box and was trying to tell him. He thinks all bad feelings must have similar origins.

His number is called at the steak sandwich place. He fetches his order and sits down again, feeling bold and adventurous, ready to give the steak sandwich a fair chance.

A shampoo bottle and a moose walk over and sit down at the table next to Pablo. The moose is the color of grapefruit juice.

Pablo takes a bite of the steak sandwich and thinks he doesn't like it. He takes the chili cheese fries out of the bag and mashes them inside the steak sandwich.

"Chili cheese fry steak sandwich," he says, feeling better. He looks at the moose and the shampoo bottle. He remembers a time in fifth grade when Bill Cardigan made fun of him for eating Captain Crunch in sausage gravy. Maybe Pablo is overweight and has unique tastes, but at least he thinks for himself. Other people tend to disagree. Other people think he is weird and wrong.

The moose and the shampoo are not paying attention to him. The moose is crying. She says, "I'm sorry the cactus died."

Anyway, Captain Crunch tastes better in sausage gravy.

The shampoo bottle is bundled in several coats, a scarf, and a sweater. Pablo wonders why. It's August, after all. Pablo takes a bite of the chili cheese fry steak sandwich. It still tastes like shit. This is one experiment that did not go as planned. He looks at the duplicate of the Transformers toy and imagines the Transformer standing up and punching the sandwich in the face.

"I'm sorry the cactus died. I am a weak human being who can't even take care of a cactus," the moose says.

"You are not a weak human being," the shampoo bottle says.

"You're so mean and critical."

What gall this moose and shampoo bottle have. Arguing in a food court. They sound just like his parents.

"I said that you're not a weak human being. How is that being critical?"

Pablo is losing his appetite. He drinks some of the smoothie, trying not to think about his parents, hoping his appetite will return.

The grapefruit-colored moose shakes her head, tears dripping down her fuzzy pink face. "No, not that. Before that, you asked me how hard can it be to take care of a stupid cactus."

"Can it be so hard?"

"You fucking asshole. You critical fucking asshole."

"I was asking a question."

"Can I ask a question?" Pablo interjects.

The moose and the shampoo bottle look at him with stunned, embarrassed expressions.

"Can't you empathize with one another for like fourteen seconds?" Pablo says.

"I am a shampoo bottle. Empathy is not one of my ingredients. It is not in my nature," the shampoo bottle says.

"Fuck nature. Fuck you," the moose says to the shampoo bottle.

"You know I really don't care that the cactus died."

"It's not always about you."

"What is wrong with you two?" Pablo says.

"We're poor," the moose says.

"We're in debt," the shampoo bottle says.

"We have no idea how we're going to survive through the winter," the moose says.

"She feels smothered because she has no friends," the shampoo bottle says.

"He is the only person I care about. It's fucked up," the moose says.

"This is so fucked up," the shampoo bottle says.

"He's depressed," the moose says.

"No, she's depressed," the shampoo bottle says.

"Are you happy with your life together?" Pablo says.

"Yes, we love each other very much," the moose says.

"We just hate ourselves," the shampoo bottle says.

"What will make you happier?" Pablo says.

"Nothing," the moose says.

"We don't know," the shampoo bottle says.

"If you're unhappy, but nothing will make you happier, and you're happy with your life together, then what is wrong?"

"We're poor."

"We're in debt."

"He can't empathize."

"She's polarizing."

Pablo thinks for a long time about what they are saying. He has never been in a serious relationship before, but he is a serious person with a serious mind. He can figure out basically any problem posed to him.

"What would Dr. Phil do?" he says under his breath.

"What did you say?" the moose says.

Pablo is a genius, but he lacks social conditioning. He does not possess Dr. Phil's stern, tough-love demeanor. He does not have a mean-ass mustache or his own talk show. In situations like these, he panics.

He panics and says, "Here you go."

He gives the Transformers toy to the shampoo bottle and the chili cheese fry steak sandwich to the moose.

"What are we supposed to do with these?" the shampoo bottle says.

"I want you to battle them," Pablo says.

"Battle them? I don't know what you're talking about," the moose says. She turns to the shampoo bottle. "What is he talking about?"

"I mean, you know, *battle*," Pablo says, patting his forehead with a napkin, feeling like the future of these strangers is in his hands. If he says the right thing, they will live happily ever after. If he says the wrong thing, everyone dies.

"I want you to pretend that the Transformer and the sandwich embody all of the bad stuff harming your relationship. Negative feelings you've harbored, unspoken annoyances, you know. Harmful debris."

"Harmful debris," the moose says. "I heard that somewhere."

"You want us to pretend that an action figure and a sandwich represent six years of harmful debris and you want us to battle them. I believe that is what you're telling us to do," the shampoo bottle says.

"We're too poor to afford any food. We would be better off eating the sandwich. Destroying a perfectly good sandwich would be wrong in our situation. We aren't privileged enough to waste food. Thank you for the offer though," the moose says.

The moose starts to slide the sandwich toward Pablo. Pablo leans over and slides the sandwich back in front of the moose.

"No," he says, "I insist."

"Will you leave us alone," the shampoo bottle says.

"I'll make you a deal. If you battle, I will give you my bunny slippers. I just bought them at the slipper store. They're blue."

"I have always wanted a pair of blue bunny slippers," the moose says.

"You can have them. You are so close to owning them," Pablo says.

"Fine, hand over the bunny slippers and we'll battle," the shampoo bottle says.

Pablo takes the bunny slippers out of his shopping bag and sets them on the table beside the Happy Meal box.

"OK, battle," he says.

The shampoo bottle drives the Transformer into the sandwich and chili cheese sauce oozes out. "Die, sandwich, die," the shampoo bottle says, imprinting a Transformer-shaped hole in the heart of the sandwich.

The moose folds the sandwich in half so that its two ends close around the Transformer like the jaws of an alligator.

"Killing me is not so easy," the shampoo bottle says.

The Transformer, held in the shampoo bottle's right hand, rips the sandwich in half.

"The Transformer has defeated the sandwich. What does this

mean? I don't know what this means," Pablo says.

"But the Transformer has not defeated the sandwich. The sandwich is immortal," the moose says.

"Prove it," the shampoo bottle says.

The moose throws steak and bread and chili cheese fries and the Transformer into the air. Cheese sauce rains down on them. A fry is stuck in Pablo's hair.

"The sandwich has chosen to self-destruct, opting out of immortality in order to defeat the Transformer."

"If they are both dead, then it must be a tie," Pablo says.

"I'm happy it was a tie," the moose says.

"I feel like we are worthy opponents," the shampoo bottle says.

Pablo wonders if this is what true love is about. Finding a worthy opponent.

The moose takes the bunny slippers and stands up. "Anyway, we have to go now. Thank you for making us battle with your sandwich and your toy. I feel better now."

"I feel okay too," the shampoo bottle says.

"We will remember this day for the rest of our lives," the moose says.

"The day all harmful debris went away," the shampoo bottle says.

"Someday there will be more harmful debris, but we will know what to do then."

"And we won't be poor so next time we can afford our own sandwich and Transformer."

"What is your name, by the way," the moose says.

"Pablo Riviera," Pablo says.

"Nice to meet you, Pablo. Thank you for improving our lives. Thank you for being the greatest human being in the history of ever," the shampoo bottle says.

The moose and the shampoo bottle walk out of the food court holding hands. Pablo sighs. He wonders if maybe he will run into them at the mall some other day. Maybe next time he will invite them back to his house to watch a movie.

The rest of his smoothie has melted, but he doesn't mind. He feels happy. Life is a good thing sometimes.

He unwraps his Happy Meal hamburger and prepares to finish his meal. Before he takes a bite of the hamburger, he reaches into his shopping bag and sneaks a mini sugar cookie out of the wax paper cookie bag. He lifts the hamburger patty, removes the pickles, and sticks the sugar cookie in the center of the hamburger, right where the pickles had been.

"I love you," he says aloud to himself, and he bites into the hamburger. He chews slowly, his belly filling with hamburger goodness, his heart fluttering in anticipation of the serious drama film about the serious historical event that he will watch by himself tonight at home. He won't have brand new bunny slippers to warm his feet, but he is glad he gave them away. Giving things to people is a sign of friendship. Pablo Riviera has friends.

He looks around the food court. The restaurants are beginning to close now.

But sugar cookies taste great on hamburgers.

And going to the mall is a wonderful thing.

CLOUD WITH A PIGSKIN HEART

I will kick your skull through the field goal posts from the fifty yard line and intercept your heart and run it back for a touchdown and spike your heart in the end zone just so my critical defensive move hurts you a little bit more.

If we face off in the Super Bowl I will kill you.
I will bleed on your helmet if you bleed on mine.
I am the cloud with a pigskin heart, motherfucker.

Rumor says my face is on a million collectable cards.
Rumor says you look retarded when I tackle you from behind.
Rumor says.

Go ahead, organize a team of your all-time greatest moments
   of love.
I will destroy your greatest moments.

My house is built out of MVP trophies so if I invite you over don't scream when I sweat Gatorade and be still when I hold you down and lick you.

Meow.

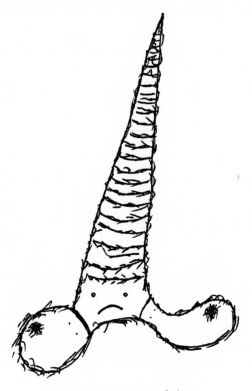

Yesterday, I grew a father.

THE GROWN FAMILY, DESTROYED

Yesterday, I grew a father.

Today, a mother in my mouth.

The mother protruded from my hard palate, buried waist-high in the bone. The mother's hair swathed my tongue like a keratin willow. Two arms pale and thin as Q-Tips pulled my tongue. Panicked grunts burbled in my throat like a garbage disposal chipping its blades on kamikaze silverware. I stretched my mouth wider and felt a ripping; the mother had a strong embrace on my tongue. I stuck a thumb and index finger in my mouth to pluck her out. She balled her hands into fists and batted at my invasive fingers. I flicked her, intending to stun. In retaliation, she bit off my tongue's tip, so I went for the tweezers.

The tweezers passed between my trembling, parted lips and seized the mother by the waist. She clawed at my teeth as I dislodged her. She writhed and beat at the tweezers. She had lidless black eyes and gill slits down her neck. I thought she might be mute.

I lowered the tweezers to the counter. The mother dragged herself along the counter by her arms. Red streaked behind her, across the tiles. Her legs were still entrenched in the roof of my mouth.

I reached into my mouth, removing her legs one at a time. Two holes remained in the wake of their removal. I tongued the wounds and set the little legs beside her. I took a Band-Aid out of a Band-Aid box, removed the wax paper backing, and applied the Band-Aid to the mother. The Band-Aid looked like a beige diaper on the crippled mother.

I left the bathroom and went into the kitchen. I took a carton of a dozen eggs out of the refrigerator and returned to the bathroom. I set the egg carton beside the mother on the counter. I plugged the drain and cracked twelve eggs into the sink. The broken shells floated like icebergs.

I opened the medicine cabinet and removed yesterday's father. I had tied him up with dental floss. I untied him now. He popped his joints and rubbed his neck, stiff from confinement. I dropped the mother in the sink. Without legs, she could not keep her head above the albumen. The father hurried to the sink and slid down the porcelain side. He dogpaddled through yolk and pushed eggshells aside, until he reached the mother. He took her under one arm and swam to the shallows. The mother pulled stringy egg matter from her mouth as the father sought an exit, but the sink was too slimy, the mother too crippled, to scale the steep embankment. The father and mother needed a child. That would make them what they'd always been. That would make them what I'd grown them to be: my family.

I took a crayon-drawn self-portrait out of my pocket. The edges were frayed because I didn't own scissors and had torn out my waxen miniature with my fingers. I submerged the double in egg, sticking it over the drain stop. The mother watched me. She looked confused. The father touched her cheek and said, "I will rescue our child." He dove into the egg and submerged himself. He surfaced empty-handed, shaking his head sadly. He took a breath and went under again. He lifted one of my paper arms. It tore away from the body. He tried again with a leg, more delicate this time, and met the same result. Frantic, he dismembered me in a desperate mission of rescue. Pieces of my body floated around him like jellyfish.

Finally he gave up, surfacing with my paper head disintegrating in his hands as the mother sobbed on the porcelain bank. The father and mother would splinter without child, but at least they could mourn their loss together, for now.

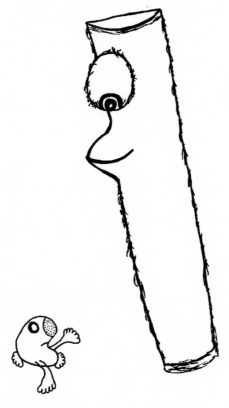

The forest had been on a morbid kick ever since.

MORBID BEAVERS

The beavers were busy painting their dam black.

The deer had recently twisted their antlers into pentagrams. The beavers wanted to show those deer who was goth. A black dam was more sinister than pentagram antlers, at least the beavers hoped.

After a few salmon attended a Bauhaus reunion concert while away on their spawning run, all the salmon had taken to wearing plastic vampire fangs. The forest had been on a morbid kick ever since.

The beavers finished painting their dam. Black paint dripped into the river and the river turned black.

Salmon heads poked up in the white-capped current. The salmon were sputtering. They spit out their plastic vampire fangs and said, "We started this, and now we've had enough. Please stop trying to be goth."

"Not goth enough to swim in a black river?" said a beaver with a sneer.

The salmon looked at each other. They always spoke as one when they spoke. "We've decided we like being plain old salmon best of all. Being goth salmon has its perks, but we miss the not-so-sinister things in life."

"Like what?" asked the sneering beaver, genuinely confused that anything that was not satanic and depressing could be meaningful. The sneering beaver had forgotten all about life before the goth days.

The salmon began listing off all the fun and beautiful things in life that were neither satanic nor depressing.

The beavers slapped their tails against the ground while the salmon listed off fun and beautiful things. The beavers felt sad and wistful, remembering all the fun and beautiful things they used to do. The salmon were right. The forest had become a much colder, crueler place when everyone turned goth.

The beavers bent down at the river's edge and began washing off the white powder on their faces, the black makeup caked around their eyes.

The salmon continued listing off all the fun and beautiful things in life. There were a lot of them, when you thought hard about it.

As the beavers busied themselves with cleaning, the deer with pentagram antlers crept amidst the trees on the other side of the river. The deer carried butcher knives and chainsaws in their hooves.

The deer leapt into the river and massacred the salmon. When all the salmon were dead, the river turned to blood.

The swift river swept the deer downstream, until they were nothing more than pentagrams in the distance, and then they were not even that.

The beavers dipped their paws into the blood and marveled at the beauty of this life-giving substance. They raised their bloody paws to the sky and threw up a great big cheer for life. It was the most fun they ever had.

STRAWBERRY AIRPLANE

So what if the birds eat all the strawberries?
I don't recall them charging us for the dream of flight,
and we will never know how many strawberries
went into the creation of every airplane alive today.

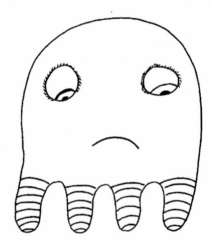

Stephen King stole your baby.

DISAPPEAR

I. The Terrible Thing

On Tuesday, the terrible thing happened.

He dropped the baking pan when she broke the news.

Enchiladas splattered across the kitchen floor. The dog barreled into the kitchen and gobbled the enchiladas. The man and the woman stared at the dog and neither of them scolded the animal. At least it was thorough and licked the floor clean.

"What was that?" the man asked, certain he'd misheard the woman when she broke the terrible news.

"I'm not pregnant anymore," the woman said.

It was true. Her stomach was no longer hard and round. Yesterday, she had been seven months pregnant. Today, nothing.

"You didn't get—" the man said.

"No, I'd never dream of it."

"What happened?"

"I woke up and found it gone, is all."

"You woke up and found it gone."

"At work, I hid in the bathroom and cried."

"Did you call the doctor?"

"I got off early and went straight away. I kept thinking there must be some mistake. The doctor is confused. He's running tests. He's calling in specialists."

The dog's chain collar was clinking against the glass baking dish, which miraculously had not shattered in the fall.

The dog rubbed its butt along the floor. The man kicked the dog and it yelped and scuttled out of the kitchen.

"You didn't need to kick the dog."

The man smelled burning and realized the oven was still on. He turned it off and stared out the window above the kitchen sink into the yard where he planned to build a tree house when the kid got a bit older.

"Can a baby just disappear?" he asked.

"No."

"Then what?"

The woman let out a gasping sound like a drowning person coming up for air.

The man waved out the window.

"Who are you waving at?" the woman asked.

"Our child. Up in the tree house. Playing."

"Don't do that. Please, whatever you do, do not act like that."

"Where do you last remember being pregnant?"

"What?"

"The logical place to begin looking is where you remember being pregnant last."

"Looking for what?"

"The baby."

"The baby? Jesus, it's not like it fell out while I was driving."

"We need to consider the possibilities."

The woman frowned in concentration.

"You said you woke up and found it gone," the man said.

"You had already left by then. I woke up and put my hands on my belly. I said good morning to our child, and then I felt the emptiness. My belly, or what it held, had disappeared."

"Lift your shirt."

"Why?"

"I want to make sure no one cut you open in the night."

"I said please don't act like that."

"We will do whatever is necessary."

"I understand, but please don't make me."

"Fine. Then what?"

"I thought maybe I'd lost my mind, temporarily. I'd slept poorly."

"You slept poorly?"

The woman shrugged. "It's hard to say. I wasn't sleeping well before the pregnancy, and now there are added complications. I should say I have not slept well in a very long time."

"So last night you slept more or less like any other night."

The woman did not answer.

"Did you have any dreams?"

The woman thought for a moment, then her eyes lit up. "I dreamed I was in *The Nutcracker*."

"Which part were you playing?"

"Every part, now that you mention it."

"You slept okay or maybe poorly, dreamed you were playing every part in *The Nutcracker*, and woke up no longer pregnant. Is there anything else I should know?"

The woman started to cry. "Do you have to interrogate me? Our fucking baby is gone and you're turning it into a police report."

"Only a few more questions now."

"It's not coming back. It's gone forever."

The phone rang. The woman moved around the center island and picked up the receiver.

"Hello?

"Oh, I understand.

"There's been what?

"Where?

"No, we'll be right there. Thank you for calling."

She hung up the phone. The quaking in her voice had ceased when she spoke into the telephone. Now she could hardly utter a word for the weeping tremors that overcame her. Between gasps, she told the man what had been said.

"The doctor said.

"There's been more cases.

"Vanished fetuses.

"We're meeting.

"With other parents.

"At the medical center.

"Tonight."

The man asked no questions. He grabbed his coat. She was still dressed in hers, having not even sat down since getting home and breaking the terrible news. They left out the front door and braced themselves against the rain that fell in cold sheets that stung. They drove away in his car. They let a talk radio pundit fill the silence until the woman turned off the radio.

The man was hunched so far forward that his chin was almost hooked over the steering wheel. Before they crossed Broadway Bridge, the man turned the radio back on. As soon as they were off the bridge, the woman turned it off again. There was absolutely no way for either of them to win.

They passed abandoned warehouses and shabby apartment complexes. They saw some people in Halloween masks standing in an empty parking lot, apparently unperturbed by the rain. Halloween was two months past.

And then they were beyond the blighted district and pulling onto the old highway that led to the medical center. From the onramp, the drive took another twenty minutes.

Living so far from the medical center had been a concern, but the doctor promised to pay a house call, if necessary, when labor day finally arrived.

They had prepared for anything, but not for this.

II. Stephen King Stole Your Baby

The doctor met them at the door of the medical center.

"Everybody else is already here. They're waiting for us in the cafeteria," he said.

Holding hands, the man and the woman followed the doctor up a long hallway dimly lit by buzzing lights.

"I want to ask you some questions," the man said.

The doctor held up a hand. "Please wait until we arrive."

When they stepped into the cafeteria, the doctor pointed to a coffee carafe and told them to find a seat among the men and women already seated in rows at the long benches. A few men and women were crying. Others' faces looked puffy from recent bouts of crying. Most held their partners in tight, uncertain embraces.

The man and the woman sat down between an arguing couple and a teenage girl who was alone.

The arguing couple hissed at each other.

"You shouldn't have smoked that one time."

"You're the one who wanted to wait."

"That has nothing to do with smoking."

"Your old sperm is the problem. Not that one cigarette."

"We needed a stable foundation."

The girl who sat alone looked at the arguing couple as if she wanted to say something. She clenched the hem of her shabby dress to prevent her hands from shaking, but they shook anyway.

The man and the woman stood and moved to another bench. They felt grateful for what they had, even though they'd just lost everything. They did not want the misery of the arguing couple and the lonely teenage girl to tarnish the little that remained.

The doctor called for attention at the front of the room. When everyone fell quiet, the only sound was the doctor swirling a wooden stick in his coffee, which he took with cream and sugar.

He set his coffee cup on top of a slide projector and picked it up again only after turning on the projector. A black circle marred the white square that lit up on the wall behind him.

"All of you came to me today with the same problem. You woke up no longer pregnant. The results are in from one of the special tests that each of you underwent today. While hard to believe, the data is irrefutable."

The doctor set his coffee on the projector again. While he withdrew a manila envelope from a briefcase, people started to shout.

"Where's our baby?"

"Why are we here?"

"Explain what's happening."

"We trusted you."

The arguing couple picked up where they had left off.

The doctor's coffee cup fell from the projector and the room went quiet once again. The doctor cursed and apologized. He said something about the night janitors needing work to do and slid a black and white image onto the slide.

"This is the uterus of a woman in this room," he said.

Everyone in the room leaned forward. The slide image was hard to make out. It appeared to be a face, but the two rings of coffee had smeared across the projector, obscuring the image.

The doctor replaced the image with another and said, "This is the womb of a different woman. She is also in the room."

The face was less obscured this time, but otherwise exactly the same.

"That's Stephen King," the woman whispered to the man.

"There must be some mistake," the man said. His eyes were fixed on the woman's belly.

"And a third womb," the doctor said, "also belonging to a woman among us tonight."

There were murmurs in the room. The man and the woman decided to be patient. They would see where the doctor was going with this.

Finally, after the doctor presented two more images featuring the face of Stephen King encased in the wombs of females in the room, the arguing couple sprang up and said together, "What the fuck is this shit?"

The doctor stared at the back wall and said, "Stephen King stole your baby."

He fled the cafeteria as the men and women began tearing each other apart.

III. Escape

The man and the woman were the only ones to survive. They watched the lonely teenage girl claw out the eyes of the arguing couple. She kissed the eyes until they melted away in her hands.

The fire alarm screamed when the man and the woman pushed through the emergency exit. Even running across the wet parking lot, they continued holding hands.

They drove away from the medical center and took the old highway to the industrial district, back across Broadway Bridge, and into the upper-middle class neighborhood where they had moved with intentions of raising a family.

They pulled into their driveway. Neither had spoken during the drive. The rain beat at the windshield and the headlights were two yolks spilling over the garage door.

The woman turned to the man and said, "We have to find Stephen King."

The man licked the sweat from his upper lip. He rarely sweated, even in hot weather, and now he was sweating in winter.

"I'll get my shotgun," he said.

He turned off the car and they went inside the house, which felt so much emptier now. The fetus had brought new life to the home. The home had been populated by their hopes and dreams of the future. Now that future was gone. What they thought was everything had disappeared, and they were left to face what had always been.

"I can't remember if I stored the shotgun in the attic or in the garage," the man said.

"Did you ever own a shotgun?" the woman asked, flicking the living room light switch repeatedly.

"Yes, I have always owned a shotgun."

"Of course," the woman said absently. She was having trouble recalling how the room was supposed to look at this time of night. There were only two settings, light and dark, and both seemed wrong.

The dog trotted into the room and the man screamed. The woman and the dog looked at him. "I thought it was something else," he said.

The woman flicked the light switch up and down, trying to remember, up and down, trying to see.

The man stuffed the dog in a closet and went out to the garage to look for his shotgun.

He returned a few minutes later, shotgun in tow.

"Let's go," he said.

The woman turned off the light forever and they went out the door.

The drive to Maine would take a few days, but they had all the time in the world.

IV. Typewriter of the Unborn

On Friday afternoon, they pulled up in front of Stephen King's house, a gothic cathedral in the heart of a middle class neighborhood.

A gardener was sculpting bushes along the walkway. The man shot the gardener in the face. The woman picked up the fallen garden shears and followed the man up to the large black doors.

The man rang the doorbell and it made a spooky ghost sound. A woman answered the door. She looked surprised.

"Who are you?" the man asked.

"I'm Tabitha King. I'm Stephen King's wife," she replied.

The man shot Stephen King's wife in the face and stepped over her crumpled body.

The woman snipped off Tabitha's nose for good measure.

"Stephen King, where are you?" the man called.

A typewriter's clatter emanated from a hallway. They walked down the hallway and stopped outside a door at the end. The typing was coming from inside the room.

The man and the woman each closed a hand over the doorknob.

Inside the room, the clink-clang of pounded keys continued. Stephen King wrote really fast.

They opened the door and stepped into the room. The man aimed the shotgun at Stephen King, who kept typing.

The woman crept up behind Stephen King and sheared off the index finger of his left hand, but even as he bled all over the keys, he kept typing. He did not even bother looking up to see who had sheared off his finger.

Alarm swelling into anger, the woman clipped away another finger, and another. She played the shears like Pac-Man until all of Stephen King's fingers were strewn around his desk like fat pencil shavings.

Despite the loss of every finger and a great deal of blood, Stephen King continued typing with his nubby hands.

"This must end," the man said. He stepped forward and blasted the typewriter.

And finally, Stephen King stopped typing. He noticed the man and woman. "Who the hell are you?" He looked at his fingerless hands and screamed.

"Shut up. We ask the questions," the man said. He forced the gun barrel into Stephen King's mouth.

"Give us our baby back," the woman said.

Stephen King pawed desperately at his ruined typewriter. The woman slapped his bloody hands away. "Give us the baby and we'll let you write your book," she said.

Stephen King tried to say something around the gun barrel.

"Shut up," the man shouted. "Nobody asked you to say a damn word."

A mewling came from somewhere close. The man and the woman turned their heads. The typewriter had grown a dozen pairs of tiny limbs. The keys were tiny, bulbous heads. Their eyes were sticky slits. Their pea-sized mouths were open, crying. The paper loader was busted open, leaking blood and little organs.

"Oh my god," the woman said.

The man fainted. He pulled the trigger as he fell. Stephen King's head-stuff made a Rorschach on the wall.

The woman pushed the corpse out of the chair and sat down at the desk. She patted her blacked-out husband on the head and hoped he'd be all right.

The keys of the typewriter cooed at her. There was blood inside their mouths. The woman stroked their slick flesh surfaces and, carefully, pressed one key down. The pressed key laughed like a baby being tickled. She pressed down on a second and a third. Then she was hammering away.

Every word she typed sent a shudder through a different jutting limb.

Perhaps before her husband woke, she could find their child. It had lived inside of her for seven months. Surely she would recognize its pulse when she pressed upon the proper key. Surely she could extract it from this new mother, this machine.

All the endless combinations must be gone through.

If she banged out every word and every phrase she knew in English, she would discover its familiar feeling. And if that proved futile, she would move on to other languages, some unknown and hardly real.

THE HAPPIEST PLACE ON EARTH

Tell me I can marry Anne Frank's skeleton.
Tell me they've lowered admission at Dachau.
Tell me Celan and Hitler learned to love.
Tell me Auschwitz was like summer camp.
Tell me the story about the violin.
The violinist died in winter in the yard.
Tell me where is Heaven, tell me who is vermin.
Tell me about the happiest place on earth.
Tell me the train to the shower for Father.
The train to the shower for Mother.
Tell me I can marry Anne Frank's skeleton.
Tell me a wedding is not like surgery.
Tell me why the bells no longer ring at church.
Tell me the saints laid down their arms.
Tell me you saw Faith in the microscope.
Tell me who am I redeeming
in the happiest place on earth.

I feel just like E.T.

MITCHELL FARNSWORTH

That was the summer we drank cheap wine and watched horror movies almost every night. We were both working shitty jobs and ignoring the debt collectors who wondered why we hadn't made payments on our student loans. I remember how it started: I was on the phone trying to explain to another debt agency that I hardly had enough money to pay rent and that the amount they were asking for would leave me homeless, when Mitchell grabbed my phone and told the person, "I'm Katie's coroner. She's dead. Don't call this number again." Then he hung up and I asked him what he'd do to me if I was actually dead. He carried me to his bedroom and we made love for the first time.

Afterward, lying beneath the sticky sheets, he asked me if I was on the pill. I told him no, but that I was good at giving myself abortions.

He looked serious and hurt and then he laughed.

I reached for my sweaty discarded t-shirt and started to wipe away the semen leaking out of me. Mitchell grabbed my hand and tossed the shirt to the floor. He stuck a few fingers in me and scraped the rest of the semen out. Soon I wanted him again, so we fucked. He pulled out and ejaculated on my belly this time. I made him lick it off with his tongue.

Exhausted and having nowhere else to be, we walked down the block to Trader Joe's and bought four bottles of their cheapest merlot. Mitchell and I had gone to the store together many times. After all, we were roommates. And yet things seemed different, now that we'd shared our most intimate places.

We ordered a pizza and proceeded to get drunk while watching the first *Alien* movie. The pizza arrived in the middle of the first chestburster scene. It sort of killed the suspense, but then Mitchell made up for it by bending me over the kitchen table and fucking me in the ass. One side of my face was rubbed raw against the hot cardboard pizza box. It was a lot more intimate than it sounds.

That night, we ate a lot of pizza, drank a lot of wine, and had a lot of unprotected sex. The next night, we did the same thing, only while watching *Aliens* instead. The night after, it was *Alien 3*. The night after, *Alien Resurrection*. I sucked his cock through the entirety of *Alien Vs. Predator* just to avoid watching the movie, even though he was limp for half of it. I drew the line at that point and made him pick a different franchise.

I can't tell you how many times I've been tit-fucked while *The Exorcist* plays in the background. Seriously, both of my boyfriends after Mitchell also wanted to tit-fuck me during *The Exorcist*. I don't know if Mitchell told them something or what. We watched that movie for like five nights straight, with Mitchell ejaculating on my chest or face several times every time we watched it. He wasn't a sexual machine, either. Normally he struggled to get a full erection after we'd fucked two or three times. Something about *The Exorcist* really turned him on. I kind of wish I asked what it was before he died.

Our routine carried on like this for three or four months. We got drunk, watched horror movies, and fucked. Sometimes we went to our shitty part-time jobs. We weren't officially dating and it was quite clear that we didn't love each other or have any illusions about a future together. That's why I wasn't hurt when Mitchell sat me down one day and told me he'd met someone at work. He told me that I should start looking for a new roommate. A week later, he moved out.

I lived alone in our apartment for another two months, until the landlord evicted me because I'd failed to pay rent. During that time, I continued watching horror movies and getting drunk. With nobody to fuck, I tried masturbating to the disturbing images onscreen. Sometimes I woke up and whatever movie I'd been watching had ended and I touched my face and felt tears.

I decided that it was probably time to get a better job and stop drinking so much. Most importantly, I decided it was time to get serious about another person.

Despite my intentions, I continued drinking and working the same job. I dated two guys in quick succession. Neither was anything special, except that they tit-fucked me while we watched *The Exorcist*.

I ended up dumping the first guy after the severity of his fetish came out. While I was fine with guys ejaculating on my face – and could even tolerate emitting a guttural "Ho, ho, ho" to bring out the full effect of my liquid beard – this guy was seriously into Santa. After our first date (pizza/cheap wine/ *The Exorcist*/tit-fuck) he flat-out refused to have normal sex with me unless he could first cum on my face and hear me say, "Ho, ho, ho." As you can imagine, we didn't last long.

The second guy was worse. He had Erectile Dysfunction. During his poor attempt to tit-fuck me on our first date (I'm not kidding about the effect *The Exorcist* had on these guys, or about my lack of creative date ideas), he smiled down at me and said in a nasally Pee-Wee Herman voice, "I feel just like E.T."

It was probably the creepiest moment of my life.

I spent another year in the city, mostly exchanging sex for a place to sleep. The guys and girls never paid me. I wasn't a slut. I guess most of them probably thought of us as an item. A few even said they loved me.

I heard about Mitchell from a young punk girl named Jasmine. We were at Movie Madness on Southeast Belmont, looking for something to rent. Movie Madness is this giant rental store that has a lot of movie props all over the place, like costumes and guns and other shit that was used on film sets. Jasmine pointed at the full-size Facehugger hanging from the ceiling and said, "My ex and I used to fuck to *Alien* all the time. The dumbass got himself killed last year."

"What was his name?" I asked, curious, but mostly just trying to be polite.

"Mitchell Farnsworth."

I wanted to tell her that Mitchell Farnsworth and I had also fucked to *Alien*, but I was too shocked by the news of his death to indulge in any sexual camaraderie.

I guess in a way I loved Mitchell, but I only found out later, much too late, when the next day I left Jasmine's place and shivered in the rain on the I-5 overpass until a trucker picked me up and offered me a ride as far south as Sacramento. I was going home to see my parents for the first time since graduating from college almost half a decade ago. I'd run my ship into the ground. I needed to see what kind of life was left for me, to find out if anyone still cared.

I never discovered how Mitchell died and I don't really remember all that much about him. We had great sex but no memorable conversations, and it's not like he knocked me up or anything. We were just two people who were bored and happened to be in the same place. And even though it's stupid and goddamn irrational, I still can't help but feel a part of me loved him. A part of me still does, even now, years later. I don't know what part of me it is. I can't explain how or why I feel the way I feel. I can only tell you that a part of me aches when I think of him, which is frequent, and it aches not for his body or his premature death. It aches for something in him that I must have sensed all along, something that's a secret part of me now, too.

REPRIEVE

Today we went to Saratoga Falls
and made our eyes
into foamy oceans

and the ballasts of our bones
cracked beneath
the saw-toothed waves

but we were safe

the way abalone
hides from the otter

We dance all the way to the grave.

MARSUPIAL

I. Where it All Ended

Call me a liar. Call me dedicated. Call me good at what I do. Call me two-faced. It's all the same to me. When I have a job to do, I do it. In the end, it's easy to forget who you're playing for, but this case I'm on now is different. I really believe in this one.

I'm eating a burrito in a deserted voodoo-themed restaurant when this guy, dressed to the nines in puffer fish leather, comes up and tells me he has a job. He says, "Come on into the back."

I stuff the last bite of burrito in my mouth and follow him. I bet Puffer Fish has heard I'm hungry for information.

We cruise through the kitchen and the chef curses us.

Through the kitchen there's a stairway that leads to a little room above the restaurant. We sit down on opposite sides of a shiny oak desk.

"I take it you're the boss," I say.

"I ain't the boss," he says.

There's a photo of two youngsters on the desk. Something like emotional heartburn pops a squat in my chest.

"These your kids?" I ask.

"Those ain't my kids," he says.

"So you ain't the boss."

"I told you I ain't the boss."

"So what's this job you got for me?"

He cracks his knuckles and pours two glasses of bourbon from a decanter on the desk.

"You afraid to die?" he asks. He slides a glass toward me.

I sniff the whiskey but don't drink it.

"What kind of bourbon is this?"

"It's imported," he says. "From Eastern Europe somewhere."

I slam down the glass. Whiskey splashes over my bare knuckles.

"Why would you buy imported bourbon?"

"I don't know. Maybe 'cause I like the taste."

"Bourbon was America's first contribution to the finer liquors of the world. You are doing a disservice to our country and all great bourbons by drinking this reindeer piss."

I stand up to go. If you want to soften up a tough guy, play hardball with him.

"What are you doing?" he wants to know.

"I'm leaving. I don't work for people who got no taste."

"Taste?" He sounds incredulous. "Taste? You think I got no taste?" He points his thumbs at the lapels of his puffer fish suit. "You think I got no taste?"

I rap my knuckles on the desk and lean over so he can smell the salsa on my breath. "This desk ain't vintage. It was bought at a discount furniture warehouse. I bet you didn't even pick it out yourself. Just strolled in flashing greens and asked them to bag up the most expensive hunk of wood they had. And your chef. The only thing worse than his attitude is his chipotle sauce."

A voice from nowhere says, "That will be enough."

The voice has hands.

It claps three times real slow.

Clap.

Clap.

Clap.

A closet door swings open and out steps a guy in a koala mask. I immediately recognize him as the real boss.

"Leonard Guest," he says, his voice muffled by the mask. "Or should I say Agent Gwin?"

"And who might you be?" I ask, racking my mind for possible slips in my act. How'd he know it was me? Did somebody rat me out?

"Call me The Marsupial," he says.

My blood freezes in my veins. There's only one way this can end, but I try to play it cool. "Marsupial, my man, call me Leonard. I go by no other name. Now tell me, why do you let your henchmen parade around in ugly suits? My grandmother could spot a joke like him a mile off."

Puffer Fish looks angry. He's still sitting in his boss's chair.

"You'd be surprised how many good men fall for him," The Marsupial says.

"They ain't that good then."

"Oh, I wouldn't say that. He's taken some of the best out of service. Your friend for instance. Jimmy the Cat."

At the mention of my undercover partner's name, I lose my cool and reach for the cigarette case in my pocket. The cigarette case that isn't there, hasn't been since I quit smoking after the car accident. "Jimmy the Cat is not dead," I say, wondering how they found us out.

"Is that so," The Marsupial says. "Would you like to see the video of his death?"

"Jimmy ain't dead. I saw him last night."

The Marsupial snaps his fingers and Puffer Fish gets up. He pulls a videotape off a bookshelf crammed with videotapes.

"Sit down, stay awhile," The Marsupial says.

I sit down, with no plans to stay awhile.

Puffer Fish loads the videotape and a flickering image appears on the wall.

It's an image of Jimmy the Cat, sitting exactly where I'm sitting now.

Puffer Fish pours two bourbons and gives one to Jimmy, who accepts and downs the lousy import in one swallow. He wipes his mouth on his sleeve and laughs like a weasel. Only there's no sound on the video. I just see Jimmy's mouth open wide and his eyes squint up in a way that can only mean one thing. I've seen guys try to lynch Jimmy over his laugh. It's loud and obnoxious and once he starts it just goes on forever. You either hate Jimmy for his laugh or you love him for it. Puffer Fish, I suspect from the gun he pulls in the video, hates Jimmy's laugh.

The video ends with Jimmy the Cat's brains on the back wall. I look over my shoulder. There's a grisly stain there. Somehow I failed to notice it upon entering.

Puffer Fish takes off his own face and I see that he's not a man. I've been conned just like Jimmy.

Some people say that death looks exactly like the thing you fear most, and they're right. That's what I'm looking at when I look into the blackness behind Puffer Fish's face. I can't tell you what it is because that's my secret. I'm holding it close.

"Kill him," The Marsupial says.

"Two questions first," I plead.

The Marsupial nods. Puffer Fish pulls out a piece, probably the same he used to off Jimmy, and trains it on me.

"I take it I don't get my questions?"

The bullet that tears off my right ear is as good an answer as any.

"Two questions is all I'm asking for," I shout. Against the pain. Against death.

"Ask 'em to God," The Marsupial says.

Puffer Fish puts the barrel to my forehead and a white light shatters my skull from within.

That thing I'm most afraid of? We dance all the way to the grave.

II. Where it All Began

Heartache fades, but it never goes away for good. I was a normal cop with a beautiful wife and two perfect kids, ages three and seven.

Then one day a drunk driver hit them on the highway and their lives were over. This was in the early days of the Death Machine. My wife and I were against it, for personal reasons more than anything. We had let the gender of both our children be a mystery until labor. We thought death should be as big of a surprise. So many people who got the test, they became obsessed. We just wanted to live our lives to the best of our ability. Knowing how we'd die wouldn't help us a bit. After the accident, a lot of people asked me why we hadn't gotten tested. I told them that no machine could have saved my family's life. I still believe that, because even when you know, you don't really know.

After my family died, I sold our house, moved into a crappy one-room apartment, and became an undercover agent. I got tested because it's a smart thing to do in this line of work. The results didn't change my outlook much. The whole thing was just entertainment. People used to ask, "What's your sign?" Now they ask, "What's your death?"

Most people get "Car Crash," or "Diabetes," or "Cancer," or "Old Age." Things like that. Rarer deaths like "Shark Attack" get a laugh. But in all my years I've never come across a death as stupid as mine: "Marsupial." Everyone in the office laughed when my results came in. They bought me a koala stuffed animal to put on my desk. That was years ago but the joke has hung around.

My opinion changed the day they put me on the Death Machine case, nearly a decade after I lost my family. I remember snidely remarking to Jimmy the Cat, "Hey, Jimmy. Run on down to the pharmacy and see if you can sneak out with their Death Machine in your pants. We'll have this case closed by lunchtime." Little did I know that there were Death Machines and then there was *the* Death Machine, the one that organized all the information culled from the others and figured out what to do with it, looking for patterns and such.

On that first day, they gave me a key to a filing cabinet full of classified files pertaining to the Death Machine.

A particular manila folder contained the information that changed my mind. It was a manifesto of sorts, written to our agency as a plea to locate the stolen machine, penned by the scientists who invented the Death Machine. This manifesto outlined their ultimate vision, which stretched far beyond the Death Machine units you find in pharmacies and doctors' offices. They recognized that the Death Machine would be processed by mass culture as a new form of entertainment. They were accepting of this because in exchange for entertainment, the Death Machine collected the most valuable thing a person has to offer: information.

I admit to not understanding most of what they said, but here's the gist: Given enough raw data, the scientists believed they could not only predict the death of everyone who would ever live, but also the times and places where deaths would occur – thereby changing the whole schema of death. The Death Machine was just the beginning, but whether the scientists' vision would ever be realized depended entirely upon the popularity of the machine. In order to save lives, they had to make the Death Machine the most popular entertainment in the world. It was well on its way when the big unit, the one that did all the fancy shit, disappeared.

I felt a duty to recover it because, well, it's my job. But there was more to it than that. If the scientists' big picture for the future was realized, then maybe some guy like me wouldn't have to lose his family in the future. This was a thing worth fighting for. This was something I could believe in, a reason to risk my life trying to recover the Machine. So here I am a week later, making this tape-recorded message while I sit in my car outside a deserted voodoo-themed Mexican restaurant. My gut feeling tells me I'll find something really big when I walk into this joint. I'd place a bet with Jimmy the Cat that I end up with the Death Machine in hand before the night is over, but Jimmy hasn't answered any of my calls today. He's probably still hung over from last night. The louse. Hey Jimmy, that's gonna be your new name from now on. Jimmy the Louse. I'm retiring to the woods when this one is over, buddy. You can come with me if you want. Or keep rotting here in the city. Your choice. If you ask my opinion, I'd say we've both been in this business long enough.

Oh, and you know how I always say I'll never tell you what I fear most? Well I'm telling you now. I'm telling this machine, anyway. Dying alone and nobody recovering my body.

Anyway, how's about a burrito? I'm fuckin' starving.

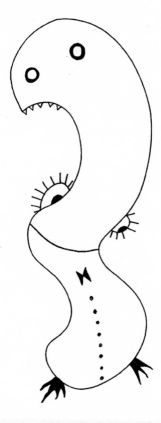

As he pulls out, he tells her that she is special.

AN ABOMINATION OF PLATYPUS

In the House of Agonies, the amputee removes his pants. He crawls onto the bed to the woman, who is tied up and could not move if she tried. He sits on her face, grinding his corncob asshole into her nose.

The amputee never sprays or splatters. His shit is consistently firm. Sometimes the woman can tell what he has eaten. Today his shit tastes like pickled radish.

She chews the shit that has dropped into her mouth. She swallows delicately, with great care. If she does not swallow delicately and with great care, he will bring in the leopard or sometimes the platypus. The platypus can do terrible things to her. The platypus is much worse than the amputee or the leopard.

The amputee turns over and jams his cock between her lips and down her throat, gagging her. She throws up a little because the amputee enjoys that. He says it makes for a more *labial* dick-suck. She does not believe he knows the definition of the word *labial*.

"Ocean trembles like jelly in a jar," the amputee tells her. He often talks while doing things to her. She sucks and throws up a little bit more because, after all, he is practically choking her. "Schmucks out there on Corinthian Island with their rich hussy wives squirting tropical punch out of their pussies. Fuckin' shriveled sagging tits blackened by the sun. These rich white women have nigger tits. Meanwhile, their husbands are becoming saints of flaccidity. Nobody to titty-fuck 'em so they got to rub on each other with slimy fish they buy at the island market. Ever been titty-fucked by a fish?"

He slips his cock out of her mouth and jabs the purple head into her eyeless socket.

"That's how it feels. Like being poked in the eye."

He plunges his cock further into the socket. Her skull aches, veins of agony branching out from the bone around the missing eye.

The platypus is responsible for removing the eye. That was a long time ago.

In a month, the amputee will chew a hole through the woman's belly and fill the wound with milk and Wheaties, then eat. He will put her body on display in the storefront window of a baby clothing store in the abandoned Pearl District. He will hide a baby shoe inside her cunt. The woman knows none of this as the amputee ejaculates into her eyeless socket.

She knows it is probably impossible, but she swears she can feel semen on her brain.

As he pulls out, he tells her that she is special.

The room downstairs off the main entryway is full of skin and teeth. The floor is made of glass. Nobody enters this room except for the platypus, and only on Sundays.

Behind the platypus's back, the amputee and the leopard call this room The Church. The platypus knows of this, for the platypus knows everything that goes on in the House of Agonies, but the platypus does not let on that he knows.

This room full of skin and teeth is where the platypus checks on his investment portfolio.

There is a computer buried under the skin and teeth. The platypus clears away a little spot and presses his face against the glass floor. There, beneath the skin and teeth and the glass floor, the computer tells him how his investments are doing. Sometimes they do well. More often, they do poorly. The platypus has no power or control over his investments. Despite frequent diggings through the skin and teeth, he has not been able to find a keyboard or a mouse in the room. His claws won't break the glass, and an invisible wall over the doorway blocks anyone or anything but the platypus himself from entering the room. He tried to drag a chair in once and it burst into flames.

On the second floor, there is the amputee and the woman's room. Sometimes the amputee calls in the leopard or the platypus to do things to the woman. Mostly they keep to themselves.

The platypus occupies the sole room on the third floor. Like The Church, nobody except the platypus goes there.

The leopard lives in the coat closet. He dreams of eating the greedy platypus, who hordes two rooms while he, a cat of the jungle, must sleep among ski poles. The coat closet is full of ski poles, despite the suspicious absence of skis. Any time the leopard moves the ski poles out of the closet, they find their way back in again. The leopard hopes to utilize the ski poles in a plot to kill the platypus and move into The Church. The leopard has never set foot on the third floor, but he estimates it to be the ideal size for a library. Yes, the leopard will move into The Church and remodel the third floor into a library to house his book. It's true. The leopard is writing a book. It is called *An Abomination of Platypus*. If only he knew how to begin.

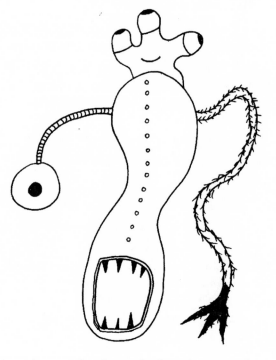

This is how my brother and I discover we are ghosts.

SKIN BLOSSOMS

Ceramic deer gnaw the skin blossoms of our paralyzed sister. She has been stranded in the garden since the middle of last week. Mother says we should not move her. If the ceramic deer fail to find food in the garden, they will break into the house and eat us. Mother tells us that our sister's flesh will regrow, if she should survive the deer feast. Anyway, she sighs, you boys are strong. Your sister is paralyzed. What kind of parent would I be to throw my most able little bodies to the beasts? No, it had to be your sister.

Another week passes. Sister dies.

Aluminum owls drop buckets full of kerosene on our house. The owls land in the garden, their eyes like handwritten death threats arriving in the mail on yellow parchment paper. They hold matches in their beaks. They strike the matches against rocks in the garden. Mother please, my brother and I beg her, but she will not leave our house behind. A captain always goes down with her ship, our mother says, Anyway you two can never leave this house because you are ghosts.

That is how my brother and I discover we are ghosts.

Our mother, not a ghost, dies in the ensuing flames. My brother believes she felt guilty over our sister's death. She needed to be absolved, he says. Is she absolved, I ask, holding hands with her skeleton. We leave her bones where they fell and take the freestanding staircase up to the second floor, where there is no longer a house, just a big open sky. The aluminum owls blink at us as if to ask, Why aren't you dead?

My brother and I go downstairs. We invent a new game. It goes like this.

One of us lies very still on the floor of ash. That one is the paralyzed sister. The other poses like Christ on the cross and stares up at the sky. Neither of us moves until an aluminum owl shits on one of us. If the shit hits the Christ mother, the mother is absolved. If the shit hits the paralyzed sister, the sister regains her ability to move and makes an angel in the ash. One day, a blue falcon shits on my brother while he is playing the mother. We decide to stop playing that game.

In the season of ceramic deer, skin blossoms appear in the garden. My brother fears that our sister has returned as a ghost. I ask why he fears her. She can live in the burnt down house with us. After all, this was a house of four. It gets lonely with only two ghost boys around.

The ceramic deer eat the skin blossoms, until the day comes when they return to the woods. Nothing magical happens. Our sister is gone forever. There is no magic in the world that can bring her back.

At night, in the hollow embrace of our mother's skeleton, we pray that everything will be fine.

IT'S NOT AN ARGUMENT
IF YOU DON'T CALL IT ONE

the walls of this apartment are made of cherry pits
and there's a man and a woman in the closet losing their skin

we have always said we will not be like them
but every night after dinner
our eyes turn red

These are not true adventures, but they are the only kind she has.

THE SEAHORSE WOMAN

The seahorse woman feels special today. She puts on lipstick and eyeliner in her abalone mirror. Hers is a natural beauty, requiring little makeup. From her closet she removes an orange dress spotted with white polka dots. This dress reminds her of the sun, which she has not seen in forty-three years. The seahorse woman is an old woman, but she remains beautiful despite the sadness of the years. Deprived of the sun for forty-three years, she has experienced much sadness. She might be happier if she could at least visit a tanning salon, or take occasional trips to tropical isles, but the seahorse woman lives in a cage, alone. Has she been imprisoned for a crime? Is she a pet in an aquarium?

She twirls and twirls. Her dress billows like a ring of orange sun around her, light as a meringue cookie. She feels special today, even though she misses her family and home. Today will offer no more than the previous forty-three years, sliced thinly into days, but she hopes, as she does every morning, that an adventure might be waiting in the dusty corners of the cage. Sometimes the adventures are frightening and sad. They tell her that her family is dead, or that she has been forgotten. These are not true adventures, but they are the only kind she has.

Dizzy from twirling, she collapses on her coral bed and waits for an adventure to come, or for the special feeling to run out, whichever comes first, whichever hurts less.

DIRTY RAG SPIRIT

Hearken that day when our caskets
open wider than the garage of a tire shop
and our dirty rag spirits pour out like automobiles
belonging to an econoline heaven.

THE ARM

I shot my brother's arm off when I was nine. We were playing with guns in the woods while our father was out. The woman we called our mother had left us the previous winter. We'd never known our real mother.

My brother and I went into the woods behind our house to play fox and hunter. We had played so many times before but nobody ever got hurt for real. I guess the difference was the gun we used, this time our father's shotgun, not a pellet gun or toy.

The kickback and loud boom scared me. The gun fell out of my arms and I ran. I went into the house and climbed inside the attic and stayed hidden there until I heard our father coming up the stairs.

Our father was a short, potbellied man with a big dark mustache. When I climbed down from the attic, he shook me by the shoulders and said, "Where's your brother?"

"Outside," I told him.

My brother and I were not permitted to go outside alone when our father was away.

He dragged me by the arm out into the yard, shouting my brother's name. I remember that no birds sang or cawed, as if they were all holding their breath.

My father squeezed my arm until I cried out in pain. He demanded to know where my brother was. I wanted to believe that what I knew to be true had never happened, that I'd not shot my brother, that he fell down at the same time the gun went off because he was so good at make-believe.

My father called his name. My brother answered this time, responding with a weak mewl that hardly sounded human. A sick deer sound.

When we came upon him, his right arm was lying next to him.

My father scooped up my bleeding brother.

"Pick up his arm," he said to me.

I picked up my brother's arm and followed my father carrying my brother back to our house.

For twenty-eight days, my brother tossed and turned in fever sleep. Without a mother to watch over him, I bore all caretaking responsibilities. I did a good job too. When our father stepped out for a few hours the day after the accident, I took my brother's severed arm out to the taxidermy shed and skinned the flesh from the bone. I buried the skin and the rest of the arm in a mound of salt. The idea was to stuff his arm the way you'd do a hog or any other wild animal. When my brother awoke, I wanted the first thing he saw to be his arm, perched like a guardian on his nightstand.

That night, my father and I were awoken by a pounding on the front door.

The door nearly broke in on its hinges as my father dressed in boots and loaded his shotgun.

"How's 'bout bear meat for breakfast?" he asked me. He grinned drunkenly as he said this, his eyes lost in the shadow glow from the bare bulb above.

I stood in the middle of the room, watching him, waiting for the arm to bust down the door, knowing it was no bear.

If it had been my brother in my place, our father would have given him a gun and allowed him first shot at whatever was beyond that door. But I was the weak and sallow one. Even by my own father, I was treated like an insect; though frail, I was not to be trusted.

He threw the door open and shot at nothing.

"Go back to bed," he said, with a suspicious sneer in his eye.

Deep down I knew my brother's severed, fleshless arm had scampered off just in time.

When I checked on the arm in the taxidermy shed the next day, I found it glowing, as if filled with fireflies. I packed on another layer of salt. If our father discovered what I was doing to the arm, he'd make me throw it out. As things stood, in his grief and confusion, he'd forgotten that he barked at me to pick up the arm. In fact, within days of my brother's accident, he refused to see him at all. He talked as if I were his only son.

The night before the first day of deer hunting season, the night before my brother opened his eyes and broke from fit and fever, my father took me out to the taxidermy shed and told me to sit down on an old wooden box, the same box in which my brother's arm was preserved. I thought he'd found me out. I felt sick. Instead, he closed his hands around mine and smiled out at me from dewy eyes.

"Tomorrow," he said, "is yours and mine."

In the absence of my brother, I'd finally become a man to my father.

The next morning before dawn, we set out into the woods.

He was swallowed by the fuzzy sea, and yet he kept on stabbing.

BLOOD GUINEAS

Ben Farr tore the guinea pig off Ben Jr. and stomped on the animal until it was no more than a puddle of fur and guts.

He tied a handkerchief around his son's bleeding neck.

"Stay with me, Benny," he said. "Talk to me."

Ben Jr. opened his mouth and blew a crimson bubble.

In another part of the house, Sharon screamed.

Ben glanced up at the wire cage on his son's desk.

The cage that used to house two guinea pigs was empty.

One guinea pig was dead. The other was . . . Sharon screamed again.

"I'll be right back, Benny. I'm going to check on your mom," Ben said, fleeing the bedroom while Ben Jr. lay on the floor, choking on his own blood.

Ben strode up the hallway toward his wife's screams. He found her in the kitchen, bashing her own face with a frying pan.

He attempted to pry the frying pan out of her hands, but she evaded his clutches and whapped him upside the head before returning the attention of the frying pan to her own face.

Sprawled out on the floor, he stared up at his hysterical wife. He wondered if she had gone insane.

And then he noticed the furry black thing on her cheek. It was the other guinea pig. Its small head was buried in her eye socket.

The guinea pig dislodged its head, clenching Sharon's left eyeball in its jaws.

Blood drizzled down her cheeks from both sockets.

Ben scrambled to his feet, taking a mental account of the weapons in the kitchen.

Settling for a steak knife, he fumbled for the knife block on the counter.

He withdrew the sharpest knife.

The guinea pig reburied its head in Sharon's left socket. Its bottom wriggled violently, as if the beast were trying to squirm all the way inside of Sharon's skull.

She dropped the frying pan and collapsed to the linoleum floor.

Ben leaned over her and grabbed the guinea pig by the tail. He pressed the tip of the knife against its haunches and drove the blade in, skewering the bloody animal.

The guinea pig shrieked infernally as it squirmed against the knife.

Ben opened the oven and tossed the impaled animal within. He turned the oven up to four-hundred degrees and exhaled a sigh of relief as the little bastard started to cook.

He picked up the telephone and dialed the police.

The phone rang and rang.

Finally, the dispatch operator took his call.

There was no standard introduction of "What is your emergency?" Instead, Ben was greeted by the shrill shrieks of a guinea pig.

He slammed the phone down.

So they'd gotten the police too.

What did this mean? Was this a local state of emergency? Was it national? He thought of all the possible causes. Terrorists. A science experiment gone wrong. Escaped military project. An uprising of the animal world. In the end it did not matter.

His wife went into convulsions. He dropped to the floor and tried to hold her steady.

She spat up blood. He wondered where it came from until she opened up her mouth and spit out a hunk of meat. She had bitten off her tongue.

She collapsed into unconsciousness.

Shortly after, she stopped breathing. Her heartbeat ceased. Ben begged her not to go, but she died anyway. He cried and held her and kissed her and cried.

The monsters had robbed him of everything.

Covered in Sharon's blood, he picked himself up from the floor and took a second knife from the block.

A knife in each hand, he moved to the front door and looked out the peephole. A lone guinea pig munched on a leaf in the middle of the yard.

He grinned. He switched both knives to the same hand and opened the door, then switched the knife back.

He stormed out of the house and across the yard, swinging his blades. The guinea pig stared at him with cold, unfeeling eyes.

He stabbed the guinea pig in the face.

Even then, its eyes held the same cold expression.

He slid his knife out of the tiny skull and stomped the dead guinea pig into the hard ground, reveling in the crunch of bones.

He sought another guinea pig to kill and spotted one approaching from down the road. He took a step toward it, but noticed that the guinea pig was followed by another, and another.

The guinea pigs, thousands of them, flooded from the neighboring houses and filled the street. He doubled back for the front door, but the door had shut and it was locked.

He turned and faced the swarm, knives out.

He would kill them all. He would kill them and have a barbecue.

The first claws and teeth dug into his flesh and were quickly followed by a thousand others.

He was swallowed by the fuzzy sea, and yet he kept on stabbing.

Knives out.

Knives out.

Dad's pancakes have never felt so much pain.

PANCAKES ARE SPOOKY

These pancakes are spooky. Dad must have made them. Whenever he makes pancakes, they somehow turn out spooky, as if he is cooking them in a graveyard instead of a frying pan.

It's Christmas morning and the three of us are sitting at the kitchen table. This is our first Christmas since Mom left us. We are doing our best to ignore her absence.

"Can you pass the syrup?" Karen asks me.

"Do you want the real maple syrup or the shitty fake stuff," I say.

"Shut up and pass me the syrup."

"Which one."

"The fake stuff," she says.

"Pass the syrup to your sister," Dad says.

I pass the bottle of Aunt Jemima to her. I have always liked Aunt Jemima syrup bottles because they are shaped like a woman.

The pancakes on my plate are howling now, like ghosts. I slather the pancakes in organic pure maple syrup and hope it will drown the pancakes' howling. The pancakes cough and sputter, but they continue to howl. They do not have mouths. They are howling through their pores.

Dad looks at me and says, "Eat your pancakes. It's Christmas."

"I'm not hungry," I say.

I do not want to tell Dad that the real reason I'm not eating is because the pancakes are spooky. He just won't understand, and after the turmoil of the past year, with Mom leaving and taking Ryan

121

with her, I am afraid to tell him that he makes spooky pancakes. Someday I will tell him, but not on Christmas. Not this year.

"Eat your pancakes or I'll slit your throat," Dad says.

Or I'll slit your throat.

That is always Dad's alternative, his only joke.

I pick up my knife and fork and cut the pancakes into little pieces. The pancakes scream like dying cats as I cut them. I drop my knife. Dad's pancakes have never felt so much pain.

"What's wrong?" Dad says.

"It's the organic syrup," Karen says. "He doesn't like it. He just wants to be cool and eat organic things."

"We'll see how organic he is when I slit his throat," Dad says.

"That's not the problem," I say. "It's the music. There's no Christmas music on. You always play Christmas music, Dad."

"I slit Christmas music's throat," he says.

Sadly, it's his only joke.

"Just kidding," he says.

He excuses himself from the table and goes into the living room and turns on the stereo and the theme song of *Frosty the Snowman* plays really loud over the surround sound speakers.

Dad returns to the kitchen table. He sits down and asks me to pass him the organic pure maple syrup.

I pass him the syrup and say, "Merry Christmas."

"It's all we can hope for," he says.

I dig my fork into the soggy mess on my plate. The pancakes are still howling, but it's hard to hear them over the Christmas music. And as I eat the spooky pancakes, I think about the alternative, like what if Mom and Ryan were still here. Would Dad's pancakes be any less spooky if they were still around? Would we be any more of a family? And the only answer is a feeling of Halloween in my belly as the ghosts of pancakes float around, waiting to be digested. And I think I hear them say, "Trick or treat."

LANTERN JAWS

My best friend's parents were in the parking lot waiting for him. Usually just his mom picked him up. Both his parents wore dark sunglasses. I knew right away something was wrong. I found out that evening. About a week later I went to his grandmother's funeral. I was excited. I had never been to a funeral. On the drive to the cemetery, my mom and dad told me it was okay to hug people in the family. The reception took place in a brassy restaurant on a golf course at the Seven Oaks Country Club. After stuffing myself with fancy food, I wandered around the golf course, wishing I'd brought my fishing pole to catch the carp that were feeding near the shore of the pond. By the time this funeral happened in my life, I had already kissed a few girls and felt pretty good about myself. A year after the funeral, my mom left my dad, my best friend and I were no longer on speaking terms, and I received a visit from his dead grandmother.

The first visitation happened before the divorce. My dad was laying into my mom pretty hard. She'd locked herself in their bedroom. He pounded on the door until she opened up, then he whipped her with a belt. I know because I heard everything. I was crying myself to sleep, face buried in the pillow, when a cold, plump figure pressed against me. I assumed it was Jasper, the fat old family cat, but Jasper did not have human hands to stroke my hair. Jasper did not have a human voice to hush my cries and promise that everything was going to be all right. In the arms of the dead grandmother, I fell fast asleep.

The next morning over breakfast, I told my mom I'd seen an angel. She kept her bathrobe clenched around her neck to hide the bruises. She asked if I was feeling okay. When I said I was fine, she told me to stop reading scary stories before bed. I finished my cereal and hurried out to catch the bus. I felt happier than I remembered feeling in a long time.

About a year later, I experienced a second visitation.

My mom and I were living alone. My grades were slipping and I was getting picked on in gym class. A teacher referred me to the school counselor due to "willful sullenness." The circle of friends I'd been a part of since third grade had finalized their excommunication of me, and I felt lost in a sea of new faces. High school was not the promised land of milk and honey I'd imagined. When I finally landed a girlfriend, she broke up with me and started seeing my old best friend, the one whose dead grandmother had visited me, in the span of a week. I spent more time by myself than ever before. My forehead broke out in zits and I smiled less often. Sometimes I bought porn from a kid named Charlie. We rode the same bus home from school. I'd bought a crumpled magazine from him on the day of the second visitation.

In bed that night, after masturbating into a sock, I was tucking my new porno mag beneath the mattress when a heavy hand fell upon my shoulder. I froze, thinking my mom had crept into the room unbeknownst to me. I wondered if she'd watched the whole scene. I turned slowly, bracing myself for the Wrath of Mom, and found myself staring into the face of the dead grandmother. Before I could scream, her jaws came unhinged like a snake's and locked down over my head, trapping me to the shoulders in a cavern of smothering, sticky blackness.

In the morning I awoke on the floor, my head sheathed in green goop. My neck and shoulders were sore. I felt weak, as if I hadn't slept at all. I climbed into bed, pulled the covers up over my head, and faked a stomachache when my mom came in to see why I wasn't up for school. I could tell she didn't believe me, but she agreed to call the school and excuse my absence.

Despite my exhaustion, I sprang out of bed the moment she left for work. I rushed out of my room. I inspected the attic entrance on the ceiling in the hallway. I'd read news stories about homeless people living in secret in attics. I ran back to my room and felt around the carpet where I'd awoken. Whatever had happened to me, I knew it was strange and terrible, and that no matter what, I could not tell my mom about it. An hour's searching yielded no results. The green stuff I'd awoken in had dried up or evaporated, but my pale pink flesh retained a sickly hue.

Growing bored and sensing an abrupt end to my adventure, I returned to bed and slept until my mom came home in the evening. Normally when I faked sick, I spent the whole day watching television, playing videogames, or looking at my nudie collection, but I felt drained. Wasted.

I dozed off during dinner after hardly eating anything. Mom started to worry that I really was sick. I worried too. She promised to call the doctor if I didn't feel better in the morning. She tucked me into bed and turned off the light. I peered into the darkness, wondering if the dead woman would return to swallow my head.

My grandfather died in Vietnam at the age of twenty-four. He used his own body to shield other soldiers from a landmine, a heroic act for which he was awarded the Gold Medal of Honor. They named part of the James Dean Highway after him. I never got a chance to meet my grandfather. My dad once told me that when he was about nine or ten, his father's ghost started sitting at the edge of his bed every night. This haunting lasted for an entire year. I hadn't seen or spoken to my father since he moved out, but I thought about him as I fell asleep that night.

*

There was a new student in first period the next morning. Her name was Vanessa Lumiere. She wore a cloth surgical mask that covered the lower half of her face, like people did in Japan when the SARS scare happened a few years ago.

After taking roll, Mr. Perone asked if any groups would be willing to let Vanessa join them on the quarter-long book analysis project, and to catch her up on the assignment. Without knowing why, I raised my hand.

"Which group are you in?" Mr. Perone asked while jotting down some notes. He wasn't even looking at me.

"*The Metamorphosis.*"

"Good." He pointed his pencil in my direction. "Vanessa, that gentleman will be your group partner. Everyone, you have the entire period to work on your projects. Feel free to work out in the hall, but keep your voices down and return by the five minute bell."

I remained seated at my desk and waited for the other students to settle down with their groups before approaching Vanessa Lumiere, who looked absorbed in the book she was reading.

Hesitant, I sat down at the desk in front of her. Up close, she was quite pretty. Olive skin, dark hair cropped short, and a slender, almost boyish frame. Still, I wondered what her face looked like beneath the mask.

"Why do you wear that mask?"

I regretted asking as soon as the words left my mouth.

She slipped the book into her bag without bothering to mark the page. "Are you familiar with *The Invisible Man*?" she asked. Her voice was muffled and far-away sounding.

"You mean the old monster movie?"

She shook her head. "No, I mean the Ralph Ellison novel."

"Oh, right. The novel." I felt myself blushing. It was just like me to assume she was referring to the monster movie and not the great American novel.

"I'm kidding," she said, laughing. "*The Invisible Man* is my favorite movie."

"Really?" I'd never met a girl who liked horror movies.

"Yeah, see, I'm sort of like *The Invisible Man*, except just part of my face is invisible. That's why I wear this mask. So nobody has to look at what isn't there."

I smiled at her, wondering if she had a boyfriend at a different school. "That's the best lie I've ever heard."

I noticed the sad gleam that passed through her eyes. I remembered that same sad gleam when some weeks later she revealed to me the terrible secret that the mask concealed.

"My name is David," I said.

"Nice to meet you, David. So what's this project we're supposed to be working on?"

I explained how at the beginning of the quarter, everyone in the class had chosen a book from a list provided by Mr. Perone, then we got into groups with the other people who chose that book. Most people chose the same book as their friends so they could be in a group together. I chose *The Metamorphosis* because it was the shortest book on the list. I was the only person who chose *The Metamorphosis*. Until that day, I'd been a group of one.

We had the entire semester to complete the four components of the project: 1) Construct/create a visual component that represents the symbolism of the book, 2) Dramatize a brief scene from the book to be presented in front of the class, 3) Chart the history of the book (including biographical details of the author, its influences, when it was written and published, what people said about it, etc.), and 4) Write a peer-reviewed seven to ten page paper on one of the major themes found in the book.

The first three components were to be completed as a group. The fourth was something we had to do on our own (we were supposed to turn in every draft of the paper we wrote to prove that peer feedback improved our writing).

"Which parts have you done so far?" Vanessa asked.

"I'm having a little trouble getting started. It's a big project even for a group of four or five people. Taking the whole thing on by myself has been a little . . . overwhelming."

"Okay, well I've already read *The Metamorphosis*, so catching up should be easy. How much longer do we have to work on it?"

I showed her the syllabus outlining the project work we were expected to do each week.

"So we're here," she said, pointing to Week Five on the syllabus. "By now you should have read the book, charted its history, and completed an outline and skeleton draft of your essay. You've already read the book, right?"

I had *tried* reading *The Metamorphosis*. I was pretty stoked that Mr. Perone's list had included a book about a guy who turns into an insect, especially considering the short length of the book. I figured it would be just like watching a movie. My excitement ended when I actually picked up *The Metamorphosis*. I liked the premise a whole lot, but the writing made me feel bored and uncomfortable, like after-school detention when they forced you to sit there with nothing, not even allowing you to do your homework. That I'd made it halfway through *The Metamorphosis* seemed like an impossible feat. Now my eyes glazed over whenever I happened to see the book, which I'd stuffed at the very bottom of my backpack.

"I'm almost finished with it," I said.

"The project is due in four weeks and you haven't even finished the book?"

"I've been swamped with Geometry homework."

This was true, although I was even more behind in Geometry.

"*The Metamorphosis* isn't even a hundred pages," she said. "If you'd read two pages a day, you would have finished it by now."

"You said you've read it."

"Yes, three times."

I wondered if this was a joke.

"My parents homeschooled me up until now. They were big on teaching me Eastern European literature, especially my dad because he came from Germany. As of last week, I've officially read every book in our home library twice, although some books I've read three or four times."

My projection of her as the "Cute Weird Girl Who Likes

Horror Movies" was shattered, replaced by a thought of *She's way too smart for me, but maybe she'll do this whole project and let me put my name on it.*

"Did you like what you read of *The Metamorphosis*?" she asked.

"I wanted to like it, but the writing . . ." I tried to formulate an intelligent way to explain that I found it boring. "It left me wanting more."

"You wanted to see Gregor Samsa eating people, terrorizing the city, and doing other monstrous things?"

"Yeah, I mean the guy turns into an insect, but he still acts like himself. It's almost like he hasn't transformed at all, except for the tough time he has getting around."

She smiled. "You went in expecting a monster movie and instead you got trapped in a room with some poor traveling salesman who hates his life."

"Exactly." I found myself nodding. "There's nothing scary about a salesman. It'd be like if a gardener turned into a werewolf, but instead of eating you, he mowed your lawn. You might be freaked out because he looks like a werewolf, but until he tries to eat you, he's still just your gardener, mowing your lawn."

Vanessa laughed. Girls never laughed at my jokes. I found myself excited to learn more about her. My mind was starting to fill in the part of her face that I couldn't see, and other parts of her as well.

"That's one way to look at it," she said. "But I think you're missing the point of the book. *The Metamorphosis* is a story about two monsters: modernity and the father. Gregor Samsa is a man who has been consumed by these monsters. Instead of killing him right off, the monsters transform him into a monster himself. Samsa is a martyr, a Christ figure. It's a parable for modern times, although Kafka's daddy issues and persecution complex obviously played a role in its creation."

"So it's a monster story, but the actual monsters aren't the ones you're reading about?" No wonder I found *The Metamorphosis* boring.

"But you *are* reading about the actual monster."

"I don't understand."

She thought for a moment. "Have you seen the movie *Alien*?"

"Yeah, it's one of my favorite movies."

"Okay, good, then you'll be able to understand. *The Metamorphosis* is a lot like *Alien*. In fact, *Alien* probably has more in common with *The Metamorphosis* than it does with any of the *Alien* sequels. If you want, you can come over to my house tonight and we can watch it. I'll point out some of the similarities, then maybe you'll enjoy the book better and we can catch up on the project."

I couldn't believe it. This cute girl was inviting me over to her house to watch one of my favorite movies. The last time a girl had asked me over to her house was in fourth grade, when Amber Tripp invited me to her birthday party (the invitation wasn't anything special, as she'd invited, no joke, every student attending Hart Elementary School).

"Yeah, sure. Where do you live?"

"Seven Oaks, off Grand Lakes Avenue. Our house backs up to the Country Club. The neighborhood is gated so if you call me when you get there I'll come out and meet you." She wrote down her number in her notebook, tore out the page, and handed it to me.

"Thanks." I folded the paper and slipped it in the pocket of my coat.

I had only been to the Seven Oaks Country Club once in my life, for the gathering after the funeral of the grandmother whose ghost had visited me twice, the more recent visit by this ghost having occurred the night before. But that's not exactly what went through my head at the time. I thought about love and the distant, impossible, yet all-pervasive prospect of sex. I thought, *She's a rich kid.*

Seven Oaks was the new neighborhood close to the high school. Most of the kids from there were Abercrombie-wearing preps. They went to youth group and got BMWs for their sixteenth birthdays. I had no problem with people like that, but I didn't belong with them either. I worried what it might mean that Vanessa's family was wealthy and mine wasn't. Hell, my family wasn't even a family anymore.

"What time should I come over?" I asked.

"Does five o'clock work for you?"

"Sure."

"Oh, wait. It's Monday. I have viol practice until six."

"You play violin?"

"No, viol. They belong to different instrument families." She continued, unfazed by my ignorance, "Is seven too late?"

"Seven works fine. That gives me time to finish my other homework before coming over." As if I would do my other homework.

"I'm glad," she said.

The five minute bell rang and Mr. Perone called everyone back to their seats. I told Vanessa that I'd see her tonight and returned to my desk.

When the passing period bell sounded, I hurried out of the classroom before anyone else. I was too excited to wait for Vanessa – and also nervous that she might change her mind about our date if I stuck around.

In second period, I spent the full hour doodling insects. Unlike Gregor Samsa, my insects were smiling and holding hands with other insects.

Since the gradual rift with my friends had widened into an irrevocable gap that made us look upon each other like hostile strangers (my ex-best friend was responsible for turning the others against me), I had taken to spending lunch breaks in the library. However, Vanessa seemed like the type of girl who would spend lunch in the library, and I was still afraid that she would come to her senses and cancel our *Alien* date if she saw me again.

My mom was meeting with her lawyer after work, so she would be home later than usual. She always hid away in her bedroom after such meetings anyway, so today was perfect for skipping out early. After second period, I'd spent the next two classes doodling more insects in love, so it wasn't like hanging around for the remainder of the day was going to benefit me. I would just go on not paying attention.

Plus, seventh period was gym class. If Vanessa happened to have gym that period, she would see me getting picked on by the jocks, particularly Frank Decker and his friend, the one they called Moose. Instead of risking embarrassment, I strolled out of the schoolyard into the parking lot. The blessing and the curse of open lunch hour was that you were free to run as far as you could, given that you returned before the bell rang. Problem was, more often than not, I did not return on time. And a day like this, I wasn't going to let some school bullshit ruin my good mood. I felt happier than I had in months.

On the long walk home, I jumped into a pile of orange and yellow leaves and basked in the October sun, something I'd not done since childhood.

Once home, I ate some food and paced around my room until it became unbearable. I expected the bike ride to take only twenty minutes, but I couldn't wait to see Vanessa. I couldn't concentrate on anything. I intended to leave early anyway because I wanted time to cool down after biking. The prospect of showing up at her fancy house as a hot, sweaty mess didn't exactly appeal to me. Before leaving, I even changed out of my favorite (though admittedly hole-ridden) jeans into the black Dockers my mom had purchased for me at the beginning of the school year. Fifteen minutes before six, I headed out on bike for Seven Oaks.

I rode through Campus Park, the distinctly middle class neighborhood where our apartment was located, across Gosford Highway, and into the outskirts of Seven Oaks.

I reached Grand Lakes Avenue quicker than expected, so I got off my bike and proceeded to walk from there. When the Seven Oaks Country Club came into view, I checked the time on my phone and realized it was only a quarter past six. I had forty-five minutes to kill.

Grand Lakes Avenue was wide and tree-lined. I wouldn't have minded biking around for a while, but I knew I would lose track of time and show up late. I decided to call Vanessa.

I reached into my coat pocket for the paper on which she'd written down her number. My right pocket was empty. So was my left. I checked my pants pockets, thinking perhaps I'd unconsciously moved the paper to one of these pockets after changing pants. No such luck. And I had no idea which of the miniature mansions backing up to the Seven Oaks Country Club might be hers. I should have saved her number in my phone, gotten her address as well, anything. How stupid could I be?

A whole lot stupider, it turned out.

I threw my bike over and kicked at the wheels, all the while spewing my favorite four-letter words in quick-fire sequences that demonstrated no shortage of creativity. Unlike many boys my age, I refrained from cursing in everyday conversation, but when I grew angry or upset, I could really let loose.

I should have stopped when the Hummer pulled up to the curb beside me. Instead, fueled by the assumption that the vehicle's driver must be some rich asshole offended by my public display of outrage – the type of rich person who would call neighborhood security and then wait around to ensure with their own eyes that security resolved the problem – I cursed louder and kicked my bicycle harder. I flipped my bike the middle finger. I did not hate rich people, but a compulsion seized me. I wanted to make myself appear obscene in front of this asshole in the Hummer. Coupled with frustration at myself over losing Vanessa's number, the presence of this Hummer caused something in me to snap.

"David, is that you?"

Vanessa's masked face poked out of the Hummer's passenger window.

I wanted to crawl into a hole and die.

"My bike's alignment is all off. I fell just before you pulled up," I lied.

"Are you all right?"

I nodded and bent over to pick up my bike in order to hide my face. I could feel myself glowing red from embarrassment. I moved stiffly to give the impression that I was still working out some kinks from the fall.

"Here, get in," she said.

She said something to the driver, who turned out to be her father. He responded in another language. German, I assumed. He sounded angry.

Vanessa said something else and the Hummer's trunk popped open.

"Put your bike in the back. My father can drive you home later."

I deposited my bike and climbed into the leather back seat. The Hummer had that new car smell. I caught a glimpse of her father's face in the rearview mirror. He was glowering.

Vanessa turned sideways in the front seat and addressed me. "My lesson ended a few minutes early today. Good timing on your part. Do you live around here?"

"It was such a nice evening, and I finished my homework early, so I decided to go for a bike ride." Here, I was reinforcing the homework lie while pairing it with another lie about my motives for coming over early.

"Are you okay? Did you fall hard?" She gave me a look of concern.

"Oh, I'm fine. No worries. How was your lesson?"

"You should get your bike fixed."

"I've taken it in before, but there's not much they can do. It's a really old bike. My dad rode it when he was my age." This part about the bike was true, at least.

The Hummer slowed. Vanessa's father leaned out of the window and punched a code into the box beside the gated entrance. The black wrought-iron gate swung open and we proceeded forward.

"I never learned to ride a bike," Vanessa said.

Vanessa's father suddenly addressed me. "What do your parents do?"

"My mom is an elementary teacher and my dad is a journalist."

He didn't respond, giving me no indication as to whether my answer satisfied or dissatisfied him.

He pulled into the pebble-embedded driveway of a brick three-story house.

Out of the Hummer, I noticed that the house across the street was made entirely of marble or granite or something.

I followed Vanessa and her father up the palm-lined walkway to the front doors, which were tall and dark. They looked heavy and hand-carved.

"Those came from a demolished cathedral," Vanessa said, pointing at the large stone gargoyles on either side of the doors.

The cold hit me once we stepped inside. It was a warm October evening, but in the house, it couldn't have been more than fifty degrees. I pretended not to notice the cold, thinking perhaps keeping the temperature low was a custom among the mega-wealthy. I didn't want to draw any undue attention to the class differences between Vanessa and me.

Her father vanished into another room without saying a word to us. To my surprise, Vanessa did not ask me to take off my shoes. On the contrary, she insisted that I keep them on. "My dad says we keep this place too clean. He says we need to give the maids something to do."

"Your dad didn't seem to like me."

"That's just how he is. Are you hungry or thirsty?"

"No thanks." I glanced at my tattered sneakers and then around at the pristine quarters the entryway led into. The place screamed professional decorator. I'd watched enough *Home and Garden Network* with my mom to know.

"I'm going to make a milkshake and maybe some popcorn for the movie. I haven't eaten since lunch. I looked around for you then but didn't see you. Where do you hang out?"

"I'm usually in the library."

"Reading Kafka, I suspect."

She laughed at her joke.

We walked through a dining room and living room, and an empty room that seemed to have no purpose, before arriving at the kitchen. The kitchen was even colder than the entryway. The goosebumps on my arms swelled to the size of peas. Vanessa, however, acted as though this frigid condition was normal, so I did the same.

I put some of my uneasiness and sense of inferiority to rest when she started bringing out milkshake supplies. The strawberries came in a clear plastic bag with the Albertson's logo. Next she removed a carton of vanilla ice cream from the freezer and it was the generic brand. I recognized the milk she took from the fridge as the discount variety my parents used to buy when we were especially poor. Despite the taste and wealth on display in every room of their house, in everything they owned, Vanessa's family shopped at the same grocery store as my parents. They even bought the cheap stuff. I don't know what I'd expected them to eat, but certainly people who drove Hummers and lived in mansions could afford more expensive food.

Vanessa caught me taking stock of the groceries. She blushed. "The maids started buying the groceries when my mom got sick."

"How is she now?"

"Getting along. Are you sure you don't want anything? It doesn't have to be a strawberry milkshake. You can have anything you want."

I was surprised how abruptly Vanessa brushed off my question about her mom. I wanted to do whatever I could to seem agreeable. "A strawberry milkshake sounds good, actually. Thanks."

She blended the strawberries, ice cream, and milk, and then stuck a bag of popcorn into the microwave. While the popcorn popped, she poured the blender's contents into two hand-cut crystal glasses, garnishing each with a colorful bendy straw.

The microwave dinged.

She opened the steaming popcorn bag and dumped the fluffy,

buttery popped kernels into a large red and white ceramic bowl emblazoned with the word POPCORN.

"I'll take the popcorn if you can carry my milkshake," she said. "We'll watch *Alien* in the basement theater. That way the noise won't disturb my mom."

I followed her out of the kitchen and down a wooden spiral staircase that descended into the basement.

A projector screen hung on the far wall. On the opposite side of the basement, the projector itself was mounted from the ceiling. Rows of actual movie theater seats occupied the space between. Floor-to-ceiling built-in shelves in the wall behind the last row of seats held hundreds, perhaps thousands, of films.

"Wow, your family must really love movies."

"My parents hate them."

"They set up all of this for you?"

She shook her head. "Oh, no. I watch maybe one or two movies a month. I have favorites that I like to re-watch, but when I put on a movie, I always get nervous and feel like I'm wasting time, so I end up turning most of them off."

"So what's with the theater?"

"My dad works in Hollywood. He gets all these free movies that none of us want, but since he's often one of the parties responsible for bringing those movies into existence, he feels obligated to keep them. Whenever he brings his business associates to the house, he makes a big deal of showing off his theater, even though he hates movies. Here." She pulled a film off the shelf and handed it to me. It was a copy of *Transformers 2*, still in the original shrink wrap.

"What does your dad do for the movies?"

I handed the movie back to her and she returned it to the shelf.

"He's an investor of some sort. I'm not really sure. He spends about one week every month in Hollywood. The rest of the time he works from home. Until my mom got sick recently, they both homeschooled me—traded off."

"So is this like his trophy shelf of movies he invested in?"

"Not at all. There's everything that has ever appeared on the American Film Institute's Top 100 list, along with some well-known foreign classics and random crap the studios send him. Then there's my favorites."

I wanted to ask what her favorite movies were, but decided that inquiring about her sick mother again would be the more sensitive and caring thing to do. "What's wrong with your mom?"

"The doctors don't know. That's why the house is so cold." A surprised look came across her face. "Oh—oh my goodness, I'm so sorry. You must be freezing. Let me grab you a blanket."

She disappeared into an alcove behind the stairs and reappeared with a checkered down comforter bundled in her arms. "I've gotten so used to the cold over the past few months. I forget how it must feel to other people." She unfolded the comforter and spread it across the middle two seats in the last row. "Well, do you want to start the movie?"

I nodded, forgetting that I'd meant to ask her about her favorite movies, and I never got a chance to ask.

We drank our strawberry milkshakes, our bodies beneath the comforter, knees and elbows touching. We had to sit very still, with the popcorn bowl balanced on my left knee and her right.

As the film started I asked jokingly if I should have a notebook and a copy of *The Metamorphosis* on hand. She shushed me and continued sucking down her milkshake. The bendy straw reached her mouth from under her surgical mask. I wanted to ask why she didn't remove the mask. We were in a dark room, after all. If she had some sort of hideous deformity that she wanted to keep hidden, I probably wouldn't get a good look at it in the flickering light of the movie screen. I decided not to say anything, content to sit in the darkened theater, enjoying the strawberry milkshake and the closeness of her warm body.

Vanessa never began explaining the similarities between *Alien* and *The Metamorphosis*. I'd half-suspected and more than half-hoped that asking me to watch *Alien* under the pretense of school work was a ploy to hang out with me, which more or less proved to be the case. The next day, however, I started reading *The Metamorphosis* from the beginning, and I finished it before the school day was out. Maybe I just wanted to impress Vanessa, or maybe she really had helped me understand the book. Either way, I enjoyed *The Metamorphosis* a lot more the second time around. I even laughed out loud at several parts.

We watched almost the entire movie in silence, until Vanessa jumped during the facehugger scene and knocked the popcorn bowl off our knees. I took her hand after that. We sat there, holding hands, until the last of the end credits rolled, then we picked up the popcorn kernels that had fallen on the floor and her dad drove me home. Vanessa walked me up to the door of my apartment and waited for me to go inside before skipping back to the Hummer, where her father sat at the wheel like a sullen rhinoceros.

The moment I stepped inside, I realized I'd forgotten to tell my mom where I was going. She was in her bedroom, as I expected. A note on the dining table said she'd left some dinner in the fridge, so she'd thought about me, though fortunately not worried. I looked in the fridge and found a baked chicken from the grocery store. I took the chicken to my room, where I devoured the entire thing, beginning and ending with a drumstick, and promptly fell asleep with a smile on my face.

I awoke in the middle of the night to discover chicken bones dancing on my face. I slapped the bones aside and cursed Jasper. I remembered that my dad had taken the cat with him when he moved out, and a lump of fear rose in my throat.

I rubbed the crusties out of my eyes and squinted into the darkness. The dead grandmother knelt on the floor, waving her hands about. Wherever she waved her hands, the chicken bones followed.

"What are you doing here?" I asked her.

She flitted her fingers and the chicken bones fell all around me. Then she looked at me with twitching, murky eyes. "So you've found true love," she said. The grin that appeared on her face was predatory.

A centipede crawled out of her nose and into her wisp of coarse black hair, which sprung out at wild angles like a bouquet of broken needles.

She spoke again: "The girl is in trouble. Bring her to me. I will fix everything."

"What do you want with her?"

"Let me be your little secret. The girl will leave you if she knows. Bring her to me. I will fix everything. Remember I'm your secret."

I awoke the next morning in a bed full of chicken bones. I'd felt pretty certain that the first two ghostly visitations had actually occurred. This one seemed more dreamlike. I'd probably forgotten to take the plastic container with the chicken bones off my bed before falling asleep, and it had come open in the night. This visitation bothered me less than the previous two. Vanessa consumed all of my thoughts. I had no space in my head for ghosts. Dream or not, the dead grandmother was right about one thing: I was better off not telling Vanessa that I'd been visited by a ghost. Maybe seeing a ghost was less weird than wearing a surgical mask around the clock, but I didn't want to risk her thinking I was some sort of freak.

I didn't think twice about the dead grandmother during the weeks that followed. Vanessa and I began studying after school together. My grades improved and teachers praised my new outlook. Vanessa and I always studied at her house, so the only evidence of my mom that I saw regularly were the empty wine bottles appearing in our kitchen trashcan with greater regularity. I told her I'd found a study friend and showed her the latest tests and homework assignments I'd gotten back. A's and B's on everything seemed to satisfy her. I continued getting picked on in gym class, but it turned out that Vanessa had a condition that exempted her from participating in physical education, so she never witnessed what the jocks did to me during seventh period and I never mentioned it to her.

Vanessa and I held hands an awful lot, but we never did more than that. This changed the night before we were scheduled to turn in our project on *The Metamorphosis* and present in front of the class. We were making final preparations on our project in one of the sitting rooms of her house, the room with all the books related to movies.

"My parents want you to have dinner with us tonight," she said.

In all the time I'd spent at her house, I had never witnessed a family dinner. Vanessa and I often made dinner for ourselves when I stayed late into the evening, but her father either ordered out or cooked his own meals. He occasionally gave me rides home. Beyond that, I saw little of him. I hadn't even met her mom. Vanessa said her mom's health was rapidly declining. It wasn't a life or death thing yet, but the outlook was grim. Whenever I asked what was wrong with her, hoping that the answer might offer some clue as to what was wrong with Vanessa (she'd still never removed the surgical mask), Vanessa iterated a version of the same unhelpful answer: "My mom can't leave the third floor of this house."

When the Westminster clock chimed seven, Vanessa's father came into the room where we were working and announced that it was time for dinner. We walked up to the third floor and paused in front of a massive armoire outside a set of French double doors.

I thought Vanessa's father was making a joke or something when he opened the armoire and, gesturing to the rusted, dome-helmeted diving suits hanging within, asked, "Have you ever been scuba diving?"

I looked to Vanessa for a clue as to how I should respond to her father's question.

"I take it you have not been diving," he said. "Vanessa, you told me he was ready for this."

I couldn't tell if he was angry or disappointed. I thought maybe it was a joke.

"He is ready, Dad. Trust me."

"Ready for what?" I asked.

"You must wear the suit if you are to eat dinner with us," her father said.

He didn't have to say it twice.

Vanessa and I donned the bulky diving suits. Her father put on only the helmet, remaining in his navy blue, wide-lapelled business suit with a goldenrod dress shirt and a silk tie patterned with a variety of golfing cats.

Her father closed the armoire and turned toward the French doors.

I shuffled into the limestone-floored, high-ceilinged room behind Vanessa and her father. The entire third floor had been converted into one large room, empty except for an aquarium. The aquarium was so large that it took up most of the available space. The only walking space consisted of four small, connecting hallways leading nowhere, leading around and around the aquarium.

"This is my mother," Vanessa said, tapping on the glass.

The lone creature within the aquarium pressed its – rather, her – face against the side of the tank. She looked exactly like a mermaid, except much older and uglier than any I'd seen in movies. Also, she had tentacles instead of arms.

"Nice to meet you," said a voice inside my head.

I looked around to see who'd spoken.

"She's telepathic," Vanessa said.

"Do you like sushi?" the mother said. Again I only heard her from within.

"I've actually never had sushi," I admitted.

She smiled warmly. "This sushi is the best. I'm sure you'll like it."

Vanessa's father removed a ladder from a closet. He pushed past me and propped the ladder against the aquarium. He looked at me sternly. "Glide in, do not splash. The maids do not come up here. We must not make a mess."

I nodded from inside my diving suit. The father kept his eyes fixed on me.

"He wants you to climb up first," Vanessa said.

I looked at Vanessa's mother again. I noticed some bandages, blood seeping through them, wrapped around her lower half.

Sushi, I thought. *We're going to eat her mother.*

I gagged a little.

"Go on then," her father said.

I climbed the ladder and slid into the cold water. Vanessa followed, then her father.

The four of us sat around a dinner table at the bottom of the aquarium. It was set like a normal dinner table.

Her mother clasped her tentacles together and bowed her head. Vanessa bowed too. I bowed as well. Her father said a prayer in German, or whatever language it was he spoke.

After the prayer, Vanessa asked me to pass the ginger, which I did.

I stared at the sushi rolls on my plate and mustered up the courage to ask her mother, "Did you make the sushi yourself?"

"No. This is from our favorite sushi restaurant, up in Monterey. For special occasions, we fly in their best chef to cook for us. He's truly a master."

"An artist," the father said.

"Yes, an artist," the mother agreed.

I picked up my chopsticks. They felt awkward in my gloved fingers. While her mother plowed through countless sushi rolls, Vanessa and her father only pretended to eat. They moved the rolls around on their plates, occasionally lifting a piece to their diving helmets, but of course it was impossible to eat. I felt relieved. I did not savor the prospect of an underwater meal, and I'd never developed a taste for seafood.

"My daughter likes you very much," the mother said.

"I like her too," I said.

"This frightens us," her father said.

I'd never been in this situation before and I fumbled for the right lines. "I'm not like most boys."

"But you are a boy," the mother said.

"You cannot rescue our daughter," the father said.

I recalled that the dead grandmother had told me Vanessa was in trouble.

"Can someone pass the wasabi?" her mother asked. "Oh, never

mind." She reached a tentacle across the table and grabbed the tiny bowl of wasabi herself. "Sometimes I forget how far these things reach."

"Our daughter is a vessel," the father said.

"Knut, you're telling him too much."

"He should know if they are dating. I will not tolerate a knight in armor. He must know that we are Vanessa's masters. He is not her master. He is not a hero."

I glanced at Vanessa. She was staring at her plate, looking painfully embarrassed.

"When the time comes for us to move inside Vanessa, will you try to stop us?" the father asked.

Vanessa bolted up in her chair despite the weight of the diving suit. "He doesn't understand," she said. "You can't ask him a question like that."

"For our safety and yours, we must make him understand," the father said.

Now the mother spoke aloud, almost shouting, in a voice much more guttural than her own: "She holds within her the sleeping city of R'lyeh. We are the original gods who dwelled there, before we were pushed out. When we have returned to our primordial forms, we shall pass through her portal mouth and retake our beloved R'lyeh."

"Stop it, Mother," Vanessa screamed. "Come on, David. You don't have to put up with this."

She engaged a flotation device on the back of my diving suit and I floated to the surface. A few seconds later, she was bobbing next to me. We climbed out of the tank, stowed the suits in the armoire, and ordered a pizza while we finished up our project.

"I'm so sorry about my parents," she said.

"No, it's okay. My family is crazy too."

"But is your mom a monster?"

"No, but my dad is."

"I like you, David."

"I like you too."

She looked stunned. "Even after all that?"

I shrugged. "Yeah, I mean nobody is defined by their parents. You're totally your own person."

She shook her head. "Sadly, I'm not."

I took her hand in mine and swallowed back a lump in my throat. "Will you be my girlfriend?"

"Are you only asking because you feel bad for me?"

"No, of course not."

"Then yes, I will be your girlfriend. Under one condition."

"What's that?"

"Will you be my boyfriend?"

We both smiled and laughed a little. We leaned in and shared our first kiss. Her face felt cold and hard beneath the surgical mask. I asked her to remove it and she said no.

The next day, we gave our presentation on *The Metamorphosis* in front of the class and scored a 48/50, the highest grade anyone received on the presentation component. We decided to go out together that night to celebrate.

We hadn't ever gone anywhere together before. We'd only spent time at her house, usually doing homework and studying.

"How about miniature golf?" I suggested.

Mini golf? Were we twelve? I immediately felt like an idiot for suggesting it, but Vanessa loved the idea. She had never been mini golfing before.

"There's a course just a couple blocks from my apartment. If you come home with me, we can walk there later. If we want to see a movie, there's a theater right across from the course."

"Okay, yeah," Vanessa agreed. "Let me call my dad at lunch and make sure it's fine with him."

As we hugged before parting for our next classes, I tried to kiss her, but she pulled away.

"I'm sorry," she said.

I felt confused, so I just turned and walked to my next class.

Neither of us brought it up when we met up at lunch hour. Her dad said it was okay for her to come home with me and we were both ecstatic about our date.

When we got on the bus to go home, the only seats available next to each other were right in front of Charlie. My stomach lurched. I worried that he was going to try and sell me porn to embarrass me in front of Vanessa. Charlie kept his mouth shut, though, and with Vanessa beside me, being on the hot and crowded bus felt somehow pleasant.

I remembered that our apartment was in ruins only after we stepped in through the front door into the kitchen. The empty wine bottles were my mom's fault. The cereal bowls half-filled with sour milk were mine. We were both at fault for the flies buzzing around, and it was the flies that bothered Vanessa the most. Her house was so clean all the time. She wasn't used to insects.

"Do you want a snack?" I asked, too ashamed to even address the miserable state of the place.

Vanessa smiled meekly and said, "No thanks."

"There's a good Chinese place by the movie theater. We can get dinner later if you want."

I could tell she felt uncomfortable. I wondered what would be the quickest way to leave again without making it obvious that I felt uncomfortable too.

"I'll just leave a note for my mom," I said. I scribbled on the dry erase board on the fridge: *Going out with Vanessa. Be home later.*

I showed Vanessa my room just long enough to dump our backpacks by the door. She didn't even step inside. I didn't want her to see or smell the chicken carcass alive with maggots in my Miami Dolphins trashcan.

We headed out of my wreck of a home to have our first official date together.

We walked over to the shopping center where there was the mini golf place, the movie theater, and a bunch of stores and restaurants. I held the door open for Vanessa to the mini golf place, but she stopped, frozen in place. "You didn't tell me it was glow-in-the-dark," she said.

"Yeah, it's 3-D, glow-in-the-dark mini golf. I know it's kid's stuff—"

"No, that's not the problem."

"Then what *is* the problem?"

"Can we do something else, please? I don't care what we do. Just not this."

"Let's go see what's playing." I kicked myself for even suggesting mini golf in the first place. She was probably too nice to turn down my idea, but then had to shut it down once she saw how lame the mini golf place actually was.

We walked across the parking lot to the movie theater and stared up at the big marquee that listed all the movies and the show times.

"Is there anything you want to see?" I asked.

"Look, David. I need to tell you something."

There was a finality in her words that sank my heart.

"Maybe it's easier if I show you. Is there someplace we can go?"

I didn't want to suggest my apartment again because of how uncomfortable she obviously felt being there, but I failed to think of anywhere else to go that would be as private.

"We could get some food and go down to the park. There's a picnic table near the duck pond that's mostly secluded by trees. Somebody might already be sitting there, but we could try."

"That would be nice." She spoke softer than usual. For the first time since we met, I was aware how much the surgical mask muffled her voice, like she was speaking through a television with fuzzy reception.

We got a bowl of barbecued pork and fried rice to share. They gave us two fortune cookies and a free medium soda. Vanessa filled the cup with 7-Up, no ice, while I picked up our order at the counter.

She had drunk almost all of the 7-Up by the time we sat down at the picnic table by the duck pond. She drank like she always did, with the straw tucked underneath the surgical mask.

She believed in opening fortune cookies before your meal. I never opened mine until the very end, when everybody else was already standing up to leave.

She set her broken cookie aside and read her fortune: "You will be invited to share an extravagant meal."

She laughed softly and said, "Looks like mine already came true. Open yours."

I told her how I felt about fortune cookies, and she lowered her gaze to the bowl of pork and rice between us.

She ate with chopsticks. I ate with a plastic fork.

"So what is it you wanted to show me?" I asked between bites.

"I feel bad for not kissing you ever. I want to kiss you and I know you want to kiss me too, and it's not fair. You deserve to know the truth."

Great. This was where she was finally going to confess that she had a secret boyfriend, maybe in another town. I pressed my thumb into the prongs of my plastic fork and accidentally broke one of them off.

"Either show me what it is or don't," I said, feeling reckless and all-too-willing to be let down.

She promptly stabbed her chopsticks into a hunk of pork where they stuck, and then she reached behind her head. I watched her fingers work at the ties of the surgical mask.

"Wait, are you . . ." I trailed off, unable to believe it.

"You have to promise not to tell anyone, no matter what. I don't care if you hate me or never speak to me again. Just please don't tell anyone."

"I won't."

Something sad and desperate flashed in her eyes. It made me feel guilty for thinking even momentarily that Vanessa had brought me here to tell me she had a boyfriend. She was more alone than I was. And now, she finally trusted me enough to share her biggest secret.

She pulled the mask away, revealing lips and cheeks of glass. It was like the mask the phantom wore in *The Phantom of the Opera*, only on the bottom of her face, and clear instead of porcelain white.

Most disconcerting of all, I could see into Vanessa's face. Miniature trees and flowers grew inside of her. They looked prehistoric. A white light no bigger than a thumbnail glowed behind her lips. It was like a tiny sun, casting little beams of light on the flora of her face, but then I noticed that the roof of her mouth was swollen and black with decay.

I flinched at the sight of it. Vanessa registered my reaction and lowered her face.

"It wasn't always this bad," she said.

"What's it doing to you?" I asked.

"Rotting me away. Someday the light will replace me, and my mother will move inside."

I understood what her father meant when he warned that she could not be saved, but I knew better. The dead grandmother could save Vanessa.

She was crying so much that she kept fumbling with the ties of the mask. I helped her tie it on and then sat down next to her and put an arm around her. She buried her head in my shoulder and sobbed.

The light behind her lips had looked so bright, but it did not shine through the surgical mask at all.

I tried to think of something that might cheer her up and decided opening my fortune cookie might do the trick.

"Want to hear my fortune?" I asked.

She nodded yes.

I broke open the cookie but there was nothing inside.

"What is it?"

"Nothing."

"What?" She lifted her head and examined the cookie in my hand. Then she wiped her eyes and laughed. "You got a blank one."

"What does that mean?"

"It means your fortune can be anything."

"Does it?"

She nodded.

I kissed her, and although I knew for certain now that her lips couldn't move, I'd swear I felt her kissing back.

We sat in silence for a while.

"Do you have any questions for me?" she finally asked.

"A ton, if you can imagine, but only one you need to answer right now."

"What's that?"

"How do you speak?"

"I've got a voice box installed in my vocal chords."

"Ouch."

She shrugged. "It's sort of like always having a sore throat, but you get used to it."

It was growing dark, so we tossed our trash in the garbage and started heading back to my apartment. We held hands as we strolled through the park.

"Now that you've revealed your big secret, I feel like I should reveal mine as well."

She turned, her eyes wide in surprise. "You have a big secret too?"

"That depends."

"On what?"

"How bad you want to see it."

She 'kissed' me on the cheek.

"Does that mean yes?"

She 'kissed' me again.

"I like this new language you've learned. You should speak it more often."

While it was easy to forget that her face was made of glass once the mask was back in place, and though her voice was as beautiful as ever, I couldn't displace the image of her festering mouth from my mind. She would be in serious trouble if the pale light spread its disease to the rest of her body. She would probably die. *The dead grandmother will help her*, I thought, as we stepped into my fucked-up version of a home.

The lights were off. My mom was either sleeping or still out. I shut the front door as quietly as possible behind us and we tiptoed to my room. If my mom was home, she was probably drunk. I'd told Vanessa that my mom had a drinking problem, but I didn't want her to have to experience that firsthand, especially considering they'd never even met before.

We made it safely to my room. I turned on some music so that our voices wouldn't seem so loud. "Sorry my room's so disgusting," I said.

"It's fine," Vanessa said, sitting down on my bed.

I went and sat down next to her.

I kissed her for a long time, my heart beating faster, unsure how to best explain that I'd been visited by a ghost, and that the ghost had mentioned her by name.

I took a deep breath. "Here's the thing. A little over a year ago, I saw the ghost of my ex-best friend's grandmother. She visited me a second time the night before I met you. And then a third time, recently."

Vanessa clenched the hem of her skirt to keep her hands from trembling. Tears welled up in her eyes. She looked terrified.

"And this ghost mentioned me," she said, knowingly.

I nodded and opened my mouth to express surprise. How did she know the ghost had mentioned her?

"I have to go." She sprang up from the bed. She grabbed her bag and reached for the door handle.

I was staring at the chicken bones in the trash, too confused to stop her from leaving, when I realized she was speaking to me.

"Can you unlock the door?"

I shook my head. "It doesn't lock."

"Well it's locked."

"I'm telling you, the door has no lock."

The stereo stopped. The light grew very bright, so bright I could see nothing, then the room went suddenly dark, as if the light had burst. Vanessa screamed.

She beat at the door and fumbled against the walls. I stood and moved straight ahead, arms outstretched, groping the blackness.

"Hello, sweets," the dead grandmother said.

Vanessa screamed again.

I could not tell where their voices were coming from. I heard them struggle, but even when I reached what had to be, *what always were*, the edges of my room, I touched nothing. No walls, no door, no material possessions.

"Vanessa!" I flailed wildly and threw myself all across the room.

Glass shattered somewhere. I tripped over something solid and braced myself to hit the ground, but even after I should have hit the ground, I kept falling.

I woke up after three in the morning. My head felt like a block of cement. I sat up slowly and realized I was sitting in a pile of broken glass and miniature trees and flowers. The light above shone down hard upon me. The window was open. A breeze rattled the blinds.

Vanessa's face had shattered, but how?

I checked everywhere for Vanessa's bag and found it gone. I called her cell phone. Either the battery was dead or she'd turned it off.

I wanted to go and get my mom, to have someone to hold onto, but I was too afraid of the off chance that she wouldn't be there. This apartment would now be too much to bear alone. Even with the ghost gone, it was too much to manage. I've no idea how I even knew the ghost was gone. Just a feeling, I guess. The dead grandmother got what she wanted. Somehow she knew I was the one who'd deliver it. Somehow, I'd let myself be tricked.

Vanessa wasn't in English the next morning. I called and texted her during every passing period without any change from the night before. I biked to school specifically so I could go by her house afterwards just in case she failed to show up. If she was in the hospital or sick or something, I wanted to know so I could be there for her.

Her dad's Hummer was not in the driveway. I propped my bike against one of the stone gargoyles and rang the doorbell. One of the maids came to the door.

"Hi, is Vanessa home?"

The maid shook her head no.

"What about Mr. Lumiere?"

The maid shook her head no. "Mr. Lumiere will not be coming back."

I pushed past her into the house. She tried to stop me but I jerked my arm out of her grasp. I dashed up the staircase until I stood outside the great armoire that contained the diving suits. As I put one of them on, the maids downstairs yelled at each other in Spanish. I tried the French doors and found them unlocked. I went inside.

At the bottom of the aquarium, Vanessa – missing the bottom half of her face – and her mother, lay in an embrace. I brought out the ladder, propped it against the aquarium's side, and climbed. I splashed into the water and sank to the bottom. The dinner table was still set up from the night we'd eaten sushi. I knelt beside Vanessa and her mother. I put my hand on Vanessa's arm and shook her. When she did not respond, I reached for her mother's tentacles. Neither Vanessa nor her mother was alive. That was the position they died in. Like my own father, Vanessa's had fled and let his family drown. They were not brave men. I decided I could never be like that. I could never let my loved ones drown.

I took a deep breath and unscrewed my ancient diving helmet. I let it float away from me. I pressed my lips into the emptiness of Vanessa's face, where the light should have been. I would breathe new life into her lantern jaws, or die trying.

A CONDENSED HISTORY OF THE TRIASSIC PERIOD

The nothosaurs developed
in the diversifying reefs
of the Permian region.
They survived on red fungi
that coated their ammonite shells.

The first askeptosaurs
made love with the vegetal nothosaurs,
and together formed
family units
known as nucleosaurs,
a prototype
for modern corals of extinction.

YOU WILL FIND YOUR WAY

Four bowls full of arrowheads in skim milk sit at their made places on the kitchen table. A bearskin rug lies beneath the table. The bear's head is mounted on the wall behind the father's spot. The father will never eat his bowl of arrowheads or sit at the table again because the father is dead, but someday he will return anyway and he'll do those things. He'll sit and eat. He'll sit and eat. Day after day he'll sit and eat. On opposite walls behind the chairs where the son and daughter would sit hang fleshed hogs, still rotting despite the years they've spent rotting. The son and the daughter will not be returning. They are alive, however. I know this for I am the mother and I view them through my crystal ball. And even though they won't return I know in my heart of hearts that someday they'll return. I make and clear the table every day. I do this because I am afraid and I want my family to return. When night comes down I feel lonely. Music dies on the bearskin rug. Gifted gifted gifted were my children. My husband was sleepless and solemn. Someday they'll all return. We'll sit down for a breakfast of obsidian arrowheads in healthy skim milk. Afterward, we'll watch cartoons. The pope might die that day. It seems the pope is always dying when we sit down on the couch to watch cartoons. *Scooby Doo* was my daughter's favorite, *Johnny Quest* my son's. I have trouble recalling the good times we spent together, but I remember the lullaby we sang to Grandma, before she vanished in the mines. *Please don't grow sick and die. Please don't grow old and die. A million miles from here, you will find your way.* These days I sing it to myself all the time because I miss my husband, I miss my kids, I miss my mom. Someday they'll all return. Until then I'll slave over meals that won't be touched. I'll be a brave soldier on the battlefield of loneliness. I'll sing myself little songs. I'll be afraid, but not for long.

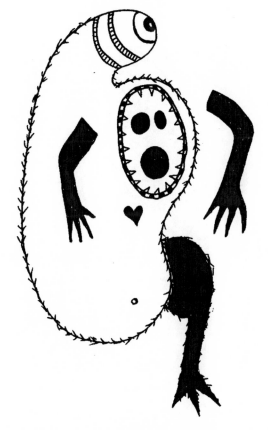

It seems the pope is always dying when we sit down on the couch to watch cartoons.

I will be a national tragedy.

THE HUMAN CENTIPEDE 2 (UFSI SEQUENCE) BY TAO LIN: A NOVEL

Martin watches *The Human Centipede (First Sequence)* on his computer then drives to the parking garage.

He sits in a tiny booth and stares at the security monitor. The screen is split four ways. A twenty-something couple walks into the upper right square. They appear to be arguing or something.

Martin picks up his tire iron and goes down to the garage.

He stands behind a concrete pillar so the boy and the girl cannot see him.

"We are so fucked," the boy says to the girl.

"Are we fucked," the girl says.

"We are so existentially fucked."

"We'll get the spare key and come back tomorrow," the girl says.

The boy pulls out his iPhone. He takes a picture of himself.

"What are you doing?" the girl says.

"I am taking a picture of myself and posting the picture on Tumblr so people remember what I looked like before my father mutilated me. This car is his life."

"Isn't that a line from *Ferris Bueller's Day Off*," the girl says.

"Maybe my book sales will go up after my father mutilates me. I will be a national tragedy."

Martin emerges from behind the pillar.

The girl looks at Martin.

Martin hits her in the head with the tire iron. She falls to the ground.

The boy's facial expression alternates between fear, anger, and sadness. He looks like the singer of Death Cab for Cutie.

Martin pulls the gun out from the waistband of his sweatpants and shoots the boy in the foot.

"You fucking asshole," the boy says.

Martin stares at the bleeding foot of the boy as if it is a Gchat message from someone he doesn't like. Martin doesn't like a lot of people. That is why he wants to build a human centipede.

He tapes the hands, feet, and mouth of the boy and girl and puts them in the back of his rapist van. He drives to a desolate part of town and parks in front of a warehouse.

Martin gets out of the van. A man who looks like Moby smokes a cigarette in front of the warehouse. The man flicks his cigarette butt and says, "Ey, let's make this quick."

Inside the warehouse, Martin gets emotional. He feels a vague surge of something like hope. He is depressed, lonely, and obese, but there is hope.

"Let's get the fuckin' lease signed," says the man who looks like Moby.

Martin imagines his twelve-person centipede crawling across the warehouse floor. He grins at the image of his grand achievement.

"Are you a goddamn retard? Let's sign the lease," the landlord says.

Martin does not like being called a retard. He shoots the landlord in the kneecap, feeling six percent closer to success.

He leaves the boy and the girl and the landlord bound and gagged on the floor of the warehouse. Now if only he can murder nine more people.

He goes home.

After feeding his pet centipede, he sits on the edge of the bed in his underwear and stares down at his bulbous gut. *There's a lonely planet inside of me*, he thinks.

He considers driving to the hardware store, getting a chainsaw, and ending it all right there in the store. Just ending it.

His mom shuffles into his room. "The doctor is here to see you," she says. She stares at Martin's computer with disdain and a high level of unease. Martin's mom believes computers are satanic. Martin stares at her until she goes away.

In the living room, Martin sits mostly naked on the couch beside the Jewish doctor, who looks like a decrepit, bearded John Lennon.

Every man looks like a famous musician to Martin. It's because his father molested him.

"Here are your pills," the doctor says, handing a bag to Martin.

"He's doing worse," his mother says.

She stands on the opposite side of the room, near the tank holding Martin's centipede. "He won't shut up about a twelve-person centipede."

"A centipede, yes," the doctor says, rubbing Martin's naked thigh in a sexual manner. "Centipedes can be a phallic symbol. Martin is expressing grief about what his father did to him."

"Because of you, my husband is in prison!" Martin's mother shouts.

"Some victims of sexual abuse mutilate their genitals" the doctor says. He works his hand further up Martin's thigh.

The doctor leaves. Martin and his mom eat dinner.

Bad techno plays loudly in the upstairs apartment.

Martin's mom stands on a chair and bangs on the ceiling with a broom.

A few minutes later, there is a knock on the front door.

His mom leaves the kitchen and returns with the upstairs neighbor, a buff tattooed skinhead. He looks like the guitarist of a metal band whose name Martin fails to recall.

"He's the one," his mother says. "He hates your music."

"You got a problem with my music?" the skinhead says.

Martin continues eating his pork and beans. He does not have a problem with this man's music. He has a problem with humanity.

The skinhead throws the flimsy kitchen table aside. He punches Martin in the face.

"Do something! Be a man like your father!" his mother says.

Martin falls out of his chair. The skinhead kicks him repeatedly. The skinhead says, "Don't ever bang on that ceiling again. You hear me, you fat fuck?"

When the skinhead leaves, Martin's mom says, "I'm going to kill us both."

Martin goes to his room. He thinks about dying while watching *The Human Centipede (First Sequence)* on repeat until he falls asleep.

The next day, Martin goes to work.

He calls the agent of Ashlynn Yennie, star of *The Human Centipede (First Sequence)*. The phone rings twice then goes to voicemail. Martin says, "This is Quentin Tarantino. I want Ashlynn Yennie to star in my new movie. Can we arrange an audition this week? Okay, have a nice day. Bye-bye now."

It is the first time Martin has spoken in months. He feels a little bit better, but not by much.

DOGS AND CATS ARE UGLY

I've worn the same boxer-briefs for about ten days in a row
    and I feel punk as fuck.
It's unnecessary to wipe your ass every time you shit.
I am clean exactly how I am.
Several times a night I run my fingers through my pubes
    and ass hairs.
I am always damp because I ride my bike all over town
and I smell my fingers and think that I have only taken
    two showers
since we last slept together.
It is like two degrees of liquid separate our genitals.
We should stop showering forever
or else forget about pulling away when we finish fucking
and sleep inside/outside each other all night long
our juices coagulating overnight
forming a thick hard web
and when we wake up in the morning we will be glued together
our pubic hair like skinny supermodels preserved in amber.
I burn up when I think about holding your hand.
I am glad your ears don't smell because I like nuzzling
    my face in your neck
and I like giving your ears wet kisses
even though I know you are grossed out by my tongue flicking
    in and out of your ears.
I am ready to marry you just say the words

and we'll go down to the doughnut shop
and we'll get married in the doughnut shop
and please remember I am just a skeleton and some canned
  food and so are you.
I want to be self-absorbed with you and tell dogs
  and cats they're ugly to their faces.
I want to celebrate Halloween with you forever.

Death is a bath towel
soiled by the bards

PUBLICATION HISTORY

Alice Blue Review, "You Will Find Your Way."

Avant-Garde for the New Millennium, "Strawberry Airplane."

The Barcelona Review, "Pablo Riviera, Depressed, Overweight, Age 31, Goes to the Mall."

Bare Bone, "Dirty Rag Spirit."

Bizarro Central, "The Arm," "Blood Guineas," and "Morbid Beavers."

Bust Down the Door and Eat All the Chickens, "Die You Doughnut Bastards."

Kill Author, "Dogs and Cats are Ugly" and "It's Not an Argument If You Don't Call it One."

The Magazine of Bizarro Fiction, "Morbid Beavers." (reprint)

Metazen, "Mitchell Farnsworth."

Metazen Christmas Special 2010, "Pancakes Are Spooky."

The Nervous Breakdown, "Three People Lose Their Genitals While Getting Naked."

New Dead Families, "Brief History of an Amputee."

New Wave Vomit, "A Condensed History of the Triassic Period," "The Happiest Place on Earth," and "The Honesty of Marsupials is a Marvelous Thing."

Nouns of Assemblage, "An Abomination of Platypus."

The Pedestal Magazine, "The Grown Family, Destroyed."

Pop Serial, "Ant Fat."

Small Doggies Magazine, "The Prisoners."

Word Riot, "Moop and the Woggle."

ACKNOWLEDGMENTS

Special thanks to Kirsten Alene, J. David Osborne, Carlton Mellick III, Rose O'Keefe, Mykle Hansen, Jeremy Robert Johnson, Bradley Sands, and all the editors who took a chance on these stories and poems.

ABOUT THE COVER ARTIST

Hauke Vagt was born in Hamburg, Germany. In 1997, he relocated to Lisbon, Portugal, where he works as a street painter and freelance illustrator.

ABOUT THE AUTHOR

Cameron Pierce (b. 1988) is the author of eight books, including *Ass Goblins of Auschwitz* and the Wonderland Book Award-winning collection *Lost in Cat Brain Land*. He has edited three anthologies: *The Best Bizarro Fiction of the Decade*, *Amazing Stories of the Flying Spaghetti Monster*, and *In Heaven, Everything is Fine: Fiction Inspired by David Lynch*. Cameron also serves as the head editor of Lazy Fascist Press.

He lives in Portland, Oregon.

BIZARRO BOOKS

CATALOG   SPRING 2012

ERASERHEAD PRESS

Your major resource for the bizarro fiction genre:

WWW.BIZARROCENTRAL.COM

Introduce yourselves to the bizarro fiction genre and all of its authors with the Bizarro Starter Kit series. Each volume features short novels and short stories by ten of the leading bizarro authors, designed to give you a perfect sampling of the genre for only $10.

BB-0X1
"The Bizarro Starter Kit"
(Orange)
Featuring D. Harlan Wilson, Carlton Mellick III, Jeremy Robert Johnson, Kevin L Donihe, Gina Ranalli, Andre Duza, Vincent W. Sakowski, Steve Beard, John Edward Lawson, and Bruce Taylor.
236 pages $10

BB-0X2
"The Bizarro Starter Kit"
(Blue)
Featuring Ray Fracalossy, Jeremy C. Shipp, Jordan Krall, Mykle Hansen, Andersen Prunty, Eckhard Gerdes, Bradley Sands, Steve Aylett, Christian TeBordo, and Tony Rauch. **244 pages $10**

BB-0X2
"The Bizarro Starter Kit"
(Purple)
Featuring Russell Edson, Athena Villaverde, David Agranoff, Matthew Revert, Andrew Goldfarb, Jeff Burk, Garrett Cook, Kris Saknussemm, Cody Goodfellow, and Cameron Pierce **264 pages $10**

BB-001 "The Kafka Effekt" D. Harlan Wilson — A collection of forty-four irreal short stories loosely written in the vein of Franz Kafka, with more than a pinch of William S. Burroughs sprinkled on top. **211 pages $14**

BB-002 "Satan Burger" Carlton Mellick III — The cult novel that put Carlton Mellick III on the map ... Six punks get jobs at a fast food restaurant owned by the devil in a city violently overpopulated by surreal alien cultures. **236 pages $14**

BB-003 "Some Things Are Better Left Unplugged" Vincent Sakwoski — Join The Man and his Nemesis, the obese tabby, for a nightmare roller coaster ride into this postmodern fantasy. **152 pages $10**

BB-004 "Shall We Gather At the Garden?" Kevin L Donihe — Donihe's Debut novel. Midgets take over the world, The Church of Lionel Richie vs. The Church of the Byrds, plant porn and more! **244 pages $14**

BB-005 "Razor Wire Pubic Hair" Carlton Mellick III — A genderless humandildo is purchased by a razor dominatrix and brought into her nightmarish world of bizarre sex and mutilation. **176 pages $11**

BB-006 "Stranger on the Loose" D. Harlan Wilson — The fiction of Wilson's 2nd collection is planted in the soil of normalcy, but what grows out of that soil is a dark, witty, otherworldly jungle... **228 pages $14**

BB-007 "The Baby Jesus Butt Plug" Carlton Mellick III — Using clones of the Baby Jesus for anal sex will be the hip sex fetish of the future. **92 pages $10**

BB-008 "Fishyfleshed" Carlton Mellick III — The world of the past is an illogical flatland lacking in dimension and color, a sick-scape of crispy squid people wandering the desert for no apparent reason. **260 pages $14**

BB-009 "Dead Bitch Army" Andre Duza — Step into a world filled with racist teenagers, cannibals, 100 warped Uncle Sams, automobiles with razor-sharp teeth, living graffiti, and a pissed-off zombie bitch out for revenge. **344 pages $16**

BB-010 "The Menstruating Mall" Carlton Mellick III — "The Breakfast Club meets Chopping Mall as directed by David Lynch." - Brian Keene **212 pages $12**

BB-011 "Angel Dust Apocalypse" Jeremy Robert Johnson — Meth-heads, man-made monsters, and murderous Neo-Nazis. "Seriously amazing short stories..." - Chuck Palahniuk, author of Fight Club **184 pages $11**

BB-012 "Ocean of Lard" Kevin L Donihe / Carlton Mellick III — A parody of those old Choose Your Own Adventure kid's books about some very odd pirates sailing on a sea made of animal fat. **176 pages $12**

BB-015 "Foop!" Chris Genoa — Strange happenings are going on at Dactyl, Inc, the world's first and only time travel tourism company.
"A surreal pie in the face!" - Christopher Moore **300 pages $14**

BB-020 "Punk Land" Carlton Mellick III — In the punk version of Heaven, the anarchist utopia is threatened by corporate fascism and only Goblin, Mortician's sperm, and a blue-mohawked female assassin named Shark Girl can stop them. **284 pages $15**

BB-027 "Siren Promised" Jeremy Robert Johnson & Alan M Clark — Nominated for the Bram Stoker Award. A potent mix of bad drugs, bad dreams, brutal bad guys, and surreal/incredible art by Alan M. Clark. **190 pages $13**

BB-031"Sea of the Patchwork Cats" Carlton Mellick III — A quiet dreamlike tale set in the ashes of the human race. For Mellick enthusiasts who also adore The Twilight Zone. **112 pages $10**

BB-032 "Extinction Journals" Jeremy Robert Johnson — An uncanny voyage across a newly nuclear America where one man must confront the problems associated with loneliness, insane dieties, radiation, love, and an ever-evolving cockroach suit with a mind of its own. **104 pages $10**

BB-037 "The Haunted Vagina" Carlton Mellick III — It's difficult to love a woman whose vagina is a gateway to the world of the dead. **132 pages $10**

BB-043 "War Slut" Carlton Mellick III — Part "1984," part "Waiting for Godot," and part action horror video game adaptation of John Carpenter's "The Thing." **116 pages $10**

BB-047 "Sausagey Santa" Carlton Mellick III — A bizarro Christmas tale featuring Santa as a piratey mutant with a body made of sausages. 124 pages $10

BB-048 "Misadventures in a Thumbnail Universe" Vincent Sakowski — Dive deep into the surreal and satirical realms of neo-classical Blender Fiction, filled with television shoes and flesh-filled skies. **120 pages $10**

BB-053 "Ballad of a Slow Poisoner" Andrew Goldfarb — Millford Mutterwurst sat down on a Tuesday to take his afternoon tea, and made the unpleasant discovery that his elbows were becoming flatter. **128 pages $10**

BB-055 "Help! A Bear is Eating Me" Mykle Hansen — The bizarro, heart-warming, magical tale of poor planning, hubris and severe blood loss... **150 pages $11**

BB-056 "Piecemeal June" Jordan Krall — A man falls in love with a living sex doll, but with love comes danger when her creator comes after her with crab-squid assassins. **90 pages $9**

BB-058 "The Overwhelming Urge" Andersen Prunty — A collection of bizarro tales by Andersen Prunty. **150 pages $11**

BB-059 "Adolf in Wonderland" Carlton Mellick III — A dreamlike adventure that takes a young descendant of Adolf Hitler's design and sends him down the rabbit hole into a world of imperfection and disorder. **180 pages $11**

BB-061 "Ultra Fuckers" Carlton Mellick III — Absurdist suburban horror about a couple who enter an upper middle class gated community but can't find their way out. **108 pages $9**

BB-062 "House of Houses" Kevin L. Donihe — An odd man wants to marry his house. Unfortunately, all of the houses in the world collapse at the same time in the Great House Holocaust. Now he must travel to House Heaven to find his departed fiancee. **172 pages $11**

BB-064 "Squid Pulp Blues" Jordan Krall — In these three bizarro-noir novellas, the reader is thrown into a world of murderers, drugs made from squid parts, deformed gun-toting veterans, and a mischievous apocalyptic donkey. **204 pages $12**

BB-065 "Jack and Mr. Grin" Andersen Prunty — "When Mr. Grin calls you can hear a smile in his voice. Not a warm and friendly smile, but the kind that seizes your spine in fear. You don't need to pay your phone bill to hear it. That smile is in every line of Prunty's prose." - Tom Bradley. **208 pages $12**

BB-066 "Cybernetrix" Carlton Mellick III — What would you do if your normal everyday world was slowly mutating into the video game world from Tron? **212 pages $12**

BB-072 "Zerostrata" Andersen Prunty — Hansel Nothing lives in a tree house, suffers from memory loss, has a very eccentric family, and falls in love with a woman who runs naked through the woods every night. **144 pages $11**

BB-073 "The Egg Man" Carlton Mellick III — It is a world where humans reproduce like insects. Children are the property of corporations, and having an enormous ten-foot brain implanted into your skull is a grotesque sexual fetish. Mellick's industrial urban dystopia is one of his darkest and grittiest to date. **184 pages $11**

BB-074 "Shark Hunting in Paradise Garden" Cameron Pierce — A group of strange humanoid religious fanatics travel back in time to the Garden of Eden to discover it is invested with hundreds of giant flying maneating sharks. **150 pages $10**

BB-075 "Apeshit" Carlton Mellick III - Friday the 13th meets Visitor Q. Six hipster teens go to a cabin in the woods inhabited by a deformed killer. An incredibly fucked-up parody of B-horror movies with a bizarro slant. **192 pages $12**

BB-076 "Fuckers of Everything on the Crazy Shitting Planet of the Vomit Atmosphere" Mykle Hansen - Three bizarro satires. Monster Cocks, Journey to the Center of Agnes Cuddlebottom, and Crazy Shitting Planet. **228 pages $12**

BB-077 "The Kissing Bug" Daniel Scott Buck — In the tradition of Roald Dahl, Tim Burton, and Edward Gorey, comes this bizarro anti-war children's story about a bohemian conenose kissing bug who falls in love with a human woman. **116 pages $10**

BB-078 "MachoPoni" Lotus Rose — It's My Little Pony... *Bizarro* style! A long time ago Poniworld was split in two. On one side of the Jagged Line is the Pastel Kingdom, a magical land of music, parties, and positivity. On the other side of the Jagged Line is Dark Kingdom inhabited by an army of undead ponies. **148 pages $11**

BB-079 "The Faggiest Vampire" Carlton Mellick III — A Roald Dahl-esque children's story about two faggy vampires who partake in a mustache competition to find out which one is truly the faggiest. **104 pages $10**

BB-080 "Sky Tongues" Gina Ranalli — The autobiography of Sky Tongues, the biracial hermaphrodite actress with tongues for fingers. Follow her strange life story as she rises from freak to fame. **204 pages $12**

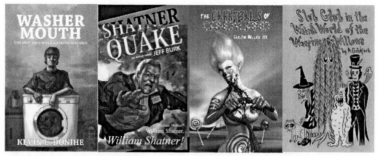

BB-081 **"Washer Mouth" Kevin L. Donihe** - A washing machine becomes human and pursues his dream of meeting his favorite soap opera star. **244 pages $11**

BB-082 **"Shatnerquake" Jeff Burk** - All of the characters ever played by William Shatner are suddenly sucked into our world. Their mission: hunt down and destroy the real William Shatner. **100 pages $10**

BB-083 **"The Cannibals of Candyland" Carlton Mellick III** - There exists a race of cannibals that are made of candy. They live in an underground world made out of candy. One man has dedicated his life to killing them all. **170 pages $11**

BB-084 **"Slub Glub in the Weird World of the Weeping Willows"** **Andrew Goldfarb** - The charming tale of a blue glob named Slub Glub who helps the weeping willows whose tears are flooding the earth. There are also hyenas, ghosts, and a voodoo priest **100 pages $10**

BB-085 **"Super Fetus" Adam Pepper** - Try to abort this fetus and he'll kick your ass! **104 pages $10**

BB-086 **"Fistful of Feet" Jordan Krall** - A bizarro tribute to spaghetti westerns, featuring Cthulhu-worshipping Indians, a woman with four feet, a crazed gunman who is obsessed with sucking on candy, Syphilis-ridden mutants, sexually transmitted tattoos, and a house devoted to the freakiest fetishes. **228 pages $12**

BB-087 **"Ass Goblins of Auschwitz" Cameron Pierce** - It's Monty Python meets Nazi exploitation in a surreal nightmare as can only be imagined by Bizarro author Cameron Pierce. **104 pages $10**

BB-088 **"Silent Weapons for Quiet Wars" Cody Goodfellow** - "This is high-end psychological surrealist horror meets bottom-feeding low-life crime in a techno-thrilling science fiction world full of Lovecraft and magic..." -John Skipp **212 pages $12**

BB-089 "Warrior Wolf Women of the Wasteland" Carlton Mellick III — Road Warrior Werewolves versus McDonaldland Mutants...post-apocalyptic fiction has never been quite like this. **316 pages $13**

BB-091 "Super Giant Monster Time" Jeff Burk — A tribute to choose your own adventures and Godzilla movies. Will you escape the giant monsters that are rampaging the fuck out of your city and shit? Or will you join the mob of alien-controlled punk rockers causing chaos in the streets? What happens next depends on you. **188 pages $12**

BB-092 "Perfect Union" Cody Goodfellow — "Cronenberg's THE FLY on a grand scale: human/insect gene-spliced body horror, where the human hive politics are as shocking as the gore." -John Skipp. **272 pages $13**

BB-093 "Sunset with a Beard" Carlton Mellick III — 14 stories of surreal science fiction. **200 pages $12**

BB-094 "My Fake War" Andersen Prunty — The absurd tale of an unlikely soldier forced to fight a war that, quite possibly, does not exist. It's Rambo meets Waiting for Godot in this subversive satire of American values and the scope of the human imagination. **128 pages $11**

BB-095 "Lost in Cat Brain Land" Cameron Pierce — Sad stories from a surreal world. A fascist mustache, the ghost of Franz Kafka, a desert inside a dead cat. Primordial entities mourn the death of their child. The desperate serve tea to mysterious creatures. A hopeless romantic falls in love with a pterodactyl. And much more. **152 pages $11**

BB-096 "The Kobold Wizard's Dildo of Enlightenment +2" Carlton Mellick III — A Dungeons and Dragons parody about a group of people who learn they are only made up characters in an AD&D campaign and must find a way to resist their nerdy teenaged players and retarded dungeon master in order to survive. 232 **pages $12**

BB-098 "A Hundred Horrible Sorrows of Ogner Stump" Andrew Goldfarb — Goldfarb's acclaimed comic series. A magical and weird journey into the horrors of everyday life. **164 pages $11**

BB-099 **"Pickled Apocalypse of Pancake Island" Cameron Pierce**—A demented fairy tale about a pickle, a pancake, and the apocalypse. **102 pages $8**

BB-100 **"Slag Attack" Andersen Prunty**— Slag Attack features four visceral, noir stories about the living, crawling apocalypse. A slag is what survivors are calling the slug-like maggots raining from the sky, burrowing inside people, and hollowing out their flesh and their sanity. **148 pages $11**

BB-101 **"Slaughterhouse High" Robert Devereaux**—A place where schools are built with secret passageways, rebellious teens get zippers installed in their mouths and genitals, and once a year, on that special night, one couple is slaughtered and the bits of their bodies are kept as souvenirs. **304 pages $13**

BB-102 **"The Emerald Burrito of Oz" John Skipp & Marc Levinthal** —OZ IS REAL! Magic is real! The gate is really in Kansas! And America is finally allowing Earth tourists to visit this weird-ass, mysterious land. But when Gene of Los Angeles heads off for summer vacation in the Emerald City, little does he know that a war is brewing...a war that could destroy both worlds. **280 pages $13**

BB-103 **"The Vegan Revolution... with Zombies" David Agranoff** — When there's no more meat in hell, the vegans will walk the earth. **160 pages $11**

BB-104 **"The Flappy Parts" Kevin L Donihe**—Poems about bunnies, LSD, and police abuse. You know, things that matter. **132 pages $11**

BB-105 **"Sorry I Ruined Your Orgy" Bradley Sands**—Bizarro humorist Bradley Sands returns with one of the strangest, most hilarious collections of the year. **130 pages $11**

BB-106 **"Mr. Magic Realism" Bruce Taylor**—Like Golden Age science fiction comics written by Freud, *Mr. Magic Realism* is a strange, insightful adventure that spans the furthest reaches of the galaxy, exploring the hidden caverns in the hearts and minds of men, women, aliens, and biomechanical cats. **152 pages $11**

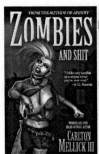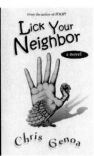

BB-107 **"Zombies and Shit" Carlton Mellick III**—"Battle Royale" meets "Return of the Living Dead." Mellick's bizarre tribute to the zombie genre. **308 pages $13**

BB-108 **"The Cannibal's Guide to Ethical Living" Mykle Hansen**— Over a five star French meal of fine wine, organic vegetables and human flesh, a lunatic delivers a witty, chilling, disturbingly sane argument in favor of eating the rich.. **184 pages $11**

BB-109 **"Starfish Girl" Athena Villaverde**—In a post-apocalyptic underwater dome society, a girl with a starfish growing from her head and an assassin with sea anenome hair are on the run from a gang of mutant fish men. **160 pages $11**

BB-110 **"Lick Your Neighbor" Chris Genoa**—Mutant ninjas, a talking whale, kung fu masters, maniacal pilgrims, and an alcoholic clown populate Chris Genoa's surreal, darkly comical and unnerving reimagining of the first Thanksgiving. **303 pages $13**

BB-111 **"Night of the Assholes" Kevin L. Donihe**—A plague of assholes is infecting the countryside. Normal everyday people are transforming into jerks, snobs, dicks, and douchebags. And they all have only one purpose: to make your life a living hell.. **192 pages $11**

BB-112 **"Jimmy Plush, Teddy Bear Detective" Garrett Cook**—Hardboiled cases of a private detective trapped within a teddy bear body. **180 pages $11**

BB-113 **"The Deadheart Shelters" Forrest Armstrong**—The hip hop lovechild of William Burroughs and Dali... **144 pages $11**

BB-114 **"Eyeballs Growing All Over Me... Again" Tony Raugh**— Absurd, surreal, playful, dream-like, whimsical, and a lot of fun to read. **144 pages $11**

BB-115 "Whargoul" Dave Brockie — From the killing grounds of Stalingrad to the death camps of the holocaust. From torture chambers in Iraq to race riots in the United States, the Whargoul was there, killing and raping. **244 pages $12**

BB-116 "By the Time We Leave Here, We'll Be Friends" J. David Osborne — A David Lynchian nightmare set in a Russian gulag, where its prisoners, guards, traitors, soldiers, lovers, and demons fight for survival and their own rapidly deteriorating humanity. **168 pages $11**

BB-117 "Christmas on Crack" edited by Carlton Mellick III — Perverted Christmas Tales for the whole family! . . . as long as every member of your family is over the age of 18. **168 pages $11**

BB-118 "Crab Town" Carlton Mellick III — Radiation fetishists, balloon people, mutant crabs, sail-bike road warriors, and a love affair between a woman and an H-Bomb. This is one mean asshole of a city. Welcome to Crab Town. **100 pages $8**

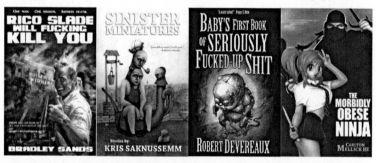

BB-119 "Rico Slade Will Fucking Kill You" Bradley Sands — Rico Slade is an action hero. Rico Slade can rip out a throat with his bare hands. Rico Slade's favorite food is the honey-roasted peanut. Rico Slade will fucking kill everyone. A novel. **122 pages $8**

BB-120 "Sinister Miniatures" Kris Saknussemm — The definitive collection of short fiction by Kris Saknussemm, confirming that he is one of the best, most daring writers of the weird to emerge in the twenty-first century. **180 pages $11**

BB-121 "Baby's First Book of Seriously Fucked up Shit" Robert Devereaux — Ten stories of the strange, the gross, and the just plain fucked up from one of the most original voices in horror. **176 pages $11**

BB-122 "The Morbidly Obese Ninja" Carlton Mellick III — These days, if you want to run a successful company . . . you're going to need a lot of ninjas. **92 pages $8**

BB-123 **"Abortion Arcade" Cameron Pierce** — An intoxicating blend of body horror and midnight movie madness, reminiscent of early David Lynch and the splatterpunks at their most sublime. **172 pages $11**

BB-124 **"Black Hole Blues" Patrick Wensink** — A hilarious double helix of country music and physics. **196 pages $11**

BB-125 **"Barbarian Beast Bitches of the Badlands" Carlton Mellick III** — Three prequels and sequels to *Warrior Wolf Women of the Wasteland*. **284 pages $13**

BB-126 **"The Traveling Dildo Salesman" Kevin L. Donihe** — A nightmare comedy about destiny, faith, and sex toys. Also featuring Donihe's most lurid and infamous short stories: *Milky Agitation, Two-Way Santa, The Helen Mower, Living Room Zombies,* and *Revenge of the Living Masturbation Rag.* **108 pages $8**

BB-127 **"Metamorphosis Blues" Bruce Taylor** — Enter a land of love beasts, intergalactic cowboys, and rock 'n roll. A land where Sears Catalogs are doorways to insanity and men keep mysterious black boxes. Welcome to the monstrous mind of Mr. Magic Realism. **136 pages $11**

BB-128 **"The Driver's Guide to Hitting Pedestrians" Andersen Prunty** — A pocket guide to the twenty-three most painful things in life, written by the most well-adjusted man in the universe. **108 pages $8**

BB-129 **"Island of the Super People" Kevin Shamel** — Four students and their anthropology professor journey to a remote island to study its indigenous population. But this is no ordinary native culture. They're super heroes and villains with flesh costumes and out-landish abilities like self-detonation, musical eyelashes, and microwave hands. **194 pages $11**

BB-130 **"Fantastic Orgy" Carlton Mellick III** — Shark Sex, mutant cats, and strange sexually transmitted diseases. Featuring the stories: *Candy-coated, Ear Cat, Fantastic Orgy, City Hobgoblins,* and *Porno in August.* **136 pages $9**

BB-131 "Cripple Wolf" Jeff Burk — Part man. Part wolf. 100% crippled. Also including *Punk Rock Nursing Home, Adrift with Space Badgers, Cook for Your Life, Just Another Day in the Park, Frosty and the Full Monty*, and *House of Cats*. **152 pages $10**

BB-132 "I Knocked Up Satan's Daughter" Carlton Mellick III — An adorable, violent, fantastical love story. A romantic comedy for the bizarro fiction reader. **152 pages $10**

BB-133 "A Town Called Suckhole" David W. Barbee — Far into the future, in the nuclear bowels of post-apocalyptic Dixie, there is a town. A town of derelict mobile homes, ancient junk, and mutant wildlife. A town of slack jawed rednecks who bask in the splendors of moonshine and mud boggin'. A town dedicated to the bloody and demented legacy of the Old South. A town called Suckhole. **144 pages $10**

BB-134 "Cthulhu Comes to the Vampire Kingdom" Cameron Pierce — What you'd get if H. P. Lovecraft wrote a Tim Burton animated film. **148 pages $11**

BB-135 "I am Genghis Cum" Violet LeVoit — From the savage Arctic tundra to post-partum mutations to your missing daughter's unmarked grave, join visionary madwoman Violet LeVoit in this non-stop eight-story onslaught of full-tilt Bizarro punk lit thrills. **124 pages $9**

BB-136 "Haunt" Laura Lee Bahr — A tripping-balls Los Angeles noir, where a mysterious dame drags you through a time-warping Bizarro hall of mirrors. **316 pages $13**

BB-137 "Amazing Stories of the Flying Spaghetti Monster" edited by Cameron Pierce — Like an all-spaghetti evening of Adult Swim, the Flying Spaghetti Monster will show you the many realms of His Noodly Appendage. Learn of those who worship him and the lives he touches in distant, mysterious ways. **228 pages $12**

BB-138 "Wave of Mutilation" Douglas Lain — A dream-pop exploration of modern architecture and the American identity, *Wave of Mutilation* is a Zen finger trap for the 21st century. **100 pages $8**

BB-139 **"Hooray for Death!" Mykle Hansen** — Famous Author Mykle Hansen draws unconventional humor from deaths tiny and large, and invites you to laugh while you can. **128 pages $10**

BB-140 **"Hypno-hog's Moonshine Monster Jamboree" Andrew Goldfarb** — Hicks, Hogs, Horror! Goldfarb is back with another strange illustrated tale of backwoods weirdness. **120 pages $9**

BB-141 **"Broken Piano For President" Patrick Wensink** — A comic masterpiece about the fast food industry, booze, and the necessity to choose happiness over work and security. **372 pages $15**

BB-142 **"Please Do Not Shoot Me in the Face" Bradley Sands** — A novel in three parts, *Please Do Not Shoot Me in the Face: A Novel*, is the story of one boy detective, the worst ninja in the world, and the great American fast food wars. It is a novel of loss, destruction, and--incredibly--genuine hope. **224 pages $12**

BB-143 **"Santa Steps Out" Robert Devereaux** — Sex, Death, and Santa Claus ... The ultimate erotic Christmas story is back. **294 pages $13**

BB-144 **"Santa Conquers the Homophobes" Robert Devereaux** — "I wish I could hope to ever attain one-thousandth the perversity of Robert Devereaux's toenail clippings." - Poppy Z. Brite **316 pages $13**

BB-145 **"We Live Inside You" Jeremy Robert Johnson** — "Jeremy Robert Johnson is dancing to a way different drummer. He loves language, he loves the edge, and he loves us people. These stories have range and style and wit. This is entertainment... and literature."- Jack Ketchum **188 pages $11**

BB-146 **"Clockwork Girl" Athena Villaverde** — Urban fairy tales for the weird girl in all of us. Like a combination of Francesca Lia Block, Charles de Lint, Kathe Koja, Tim Burton, and Hayao Miyazaki, her stories are cute, kinky, edgy, magical, provocative, and strange, full of poetic imagery and vicious sexuality. **160 pages $10**

BB-147 **"Armadillo Fists" Carlton Mellick III** — A weird-as-hell gangster story set in a world where people drive giant mechanical dinosaurs instead of cars. **168 pages $11**

BB-148 **"Gargoyle Girls of Spider Island" Cameron Pierce** — Four college seniors venture out into open waters for the tropical party weekend of a lifetime. Instead of a teenage sex fantasy, they find themselves in a nightmare of pirates, sharks, and sex-crazed monsters. **100 pages $8**

BB-149 **"The Handsome Squirm" by Carlton Mellick III** — Like Franz Kafka's *The Trial* meets an erotic body horror version of *The Blob*. **158 pages $11**

BB-150 **"Tentacle Death Trip" Jordan Krall** — It's *Death Race 2000* meets H. P. Lovecraft in bizarro author Jordan Krall's best and most suspenseful work to date. **224 pages $12**

BB-151 **"The Obese" Nick Antosca** — Like Alfred Hitchcock's *The Birds*... but with obese people. **108 pages $10**

BB-152 **"All-Monster Action!" Cody Goodfellow** — The world gave him a blank check and a demand: Create giant monsters to fight our wars. But Dr. Otaku was not satisfied with mere chaos and mass destruction.... **216 pages $12**

BB-153 **"Ugly Heaven" Carlton Mellick III** — Heaven is no longer a paradise. It was once a blissful utopia full of wonders far beyond human comprehension. But the afterlife is now in ruins. It has become an ugly, lonely wasteland populated by strange monstrous beasts, masturbating angels, and sad man-like beings wallowing in the remains of the once-great Kingdom of God. **106 pages $8**

BB-154 **"Space Walrus" Kevin L. Donihe** — Walter is supposed to go where no walrus has ever gone before, but all this astronaut walrus really wants is to take it easy on the intense training, escape the chimpanzee bullies, and win the love of his human trainer Dr. Stephanie. **160 pages $11**

CPSIA information can be obtained at www.ICGtesting.com
Printed in the USA
BVOW01s1354290616

453899BV00001B/40/P